Z-BURBIA 3
ESTATE OF THE DEAD

JAKE BIBLE

Foreword

It's interesting how a series progresses. When I wrote the first book in the Z-Burbia series, I figured it would be a satiric take on suburban life against the backdrop of a zombie apocalypse. I mean, we all have that story in us, am I right? However, as the series moved on, and I now release book three, I realize that no matter how satirical I want to be the fact is that during the zombie apocalypse, people's lives are ruined, families destroyed, loved ones lost, enemies killed. Not always the funniest backdrop.

So, the series has grown darker with each book and this one is no exception. I tried to keep the tone light where I could, but the story takes ya where it takes ya. That being said, I think this is my favorite book of the series. Why? Two words: cannibal savant. Or one word: Elsbeth.

This is her story, in a way. In fact, if you look at the other books carefully, you'll see that the series so far has actually been her story. Sure, that snarky SOB, Jace Stanford, has been narrating and hogging the spotlight, but he wouldn't have a spotlight without her. She saves his smart ass time and time again. No different in Z3.

Z-Burbia 3: Estate Of The Dead will cap the Asheville story arc. It won't be the last Z-Burbia book by far, but it will give some closure to what's been building in the last two books. That leaves room for the narrative to move along in the world. I have a feeling Z4 will be back to the snark; kinda a psychological reboot. So think of Z1-Z3 as one long movie in three acts. Z3 is the climax (hee, hee, hee, I said climax). And, boy howdy, is it ever! Enjoy!

Cheers,
Jake
January 2014

PS- When you get to the end, don't hate me. I'm a sucker for drama. More is coming!

CHAPTER ONE

Z-Day.

"Echo Team set?"

"Set."

"Bravo Team set?"

"Boots down and ready."

"Just say set."

"Set."

"Cadillac Team set?"

"Set."

"Alpha Team is in place," Foster says. "On my mark we take the facility. Keep it tight and go for body shots. We don't know who is hostile and who is just caught up in this. The job is to rescue the targets, not kill the staff."

"Roger."

"Roger."

"Copy that."

Foster holds up a fist and then three fingers. She drops one, two and three.

"Mark. We are a go!"

Her Alpha Team of private military contractors, decked out in black body armor and night vision goggles, M-4s to their shoulders, rush to the side door that their point man just blew. Foster, a woman of average height and build, but with piercing, ice blue eyes behind her goggles, pivots left then right as she is the first through the door. She steps left and the teammate behind her follows and steps right. They clear the room and keep moving.

Over their radio coms, they hear more doors being blown, then gunfire as one of the Teams makes contact.

"Report!" Foster shouts.

"Three security guards are down," Joseph "Joe T" Tennant, commander of Echo Team, responds. "But we have more coming."

"Position?" Foster asks as she moves from the first room and into the second. The rooms are paneled in faux wood with thrift shop desks and file cabinets pushed up against the walls. Foster knows the facility cost millions to build and wonders where that money went.

"We are in the west corridor," Joe T replies. "This place looks like a set from the '70s. I thought we were going up against high tech and shit. I see nothing but a Rockford Files set here."

"It's a front," Foster says. "Stay alert and keep moving. Look for the way below."

The Teams came in on foot, knowing a helicopter drop would have alerted their target to their presence. Hiking through two valleys, they came upon the unassuming modular building tucked up against the hillside in the Blue Ridge Mountains. Foster knew it was only the entryway to a facility much larger that was burrowed below or into the hillside itself. Recon intel had shown her that.

But it hadn't shown her how to get into the main facility where her targets were being held.

"This is not ideal," Hank Zorn, head of Bravo Team, says. "We are being led like rats in a maze."

More gunfire erupts over the com. Then voices shouting and a large explosion rocks the facility.

"Who was that?" Foster cries, as she starts sprinting from faux paneled room to faux paneled room. "Was that our demo?"

"Negative!" Joe T yells. "Cadillac Team is down! I repeat! Cadillac Team is down!"

"Shit," Foster grunts as she comes around a corner and face to face with Zorn. "What the fuck?"

"This is messed up, boss," Zorn says as the rest of his Team come up behind him. "Are the fucking walls moving?"

"Shit," Foster says again as she looks at the floor. She can see the gouges and scuffs made by heavy objects. Heavy objects like walls. "Mother fuck. They are moving. We're being played! I want gloves off, people! Blow these fucking walls and shoot to kill!"

"Hello there, friends," a voice crackles over speakers set into the ceiling. "It was only a matter of time before you came for us. The 1% of the 1% don't like it when their lineage is threatened. I was going to return the young ladies, with some modifications, but it looks like you have pushed my hand on this. I hold no guilt over my actions. Deep breaths and good byes."

Mist starts to flow down from holes next to the speakers and the Teams react by yanking off their goggles and pulling on facemasks.

"Gas," Foster says. "Nice."

Two explosions shake the building and a high-pitched wailing fills the air.

"We have access, boss!" Joe T shouts over the com. "Heading deeper into the hillside."

"Location?" Foster yells.

"Fuck if I know!' Joe T replies. "We just started blowing walls until we got through! Compass says we are facing northwest."

Foster turns that way and points at the wall. Two men strip adhesive from four explosive packs and jam them against the wall. Everyone takes what cover they can, arms wrapped over heads, faces tucked between knees.

BOOM! BOOM! BOOM! BOOM!

The wall is almost vaporized and Foster finds herself staring into the shocked and bleeding faces of several lab techs. Some stand there staring at the private contractors, others lay sprawled across the stainless steel floor or the lab tables that are knocked askew. No one moves as all eyes are on the rifle barrels and the soldiers for hire that pour into the room.

"The girls!" Foster shouts. "Where are the girls?"

A woman starts to speak, but then her eyes bulge and pink foam flows from her mouth. She convulses and drops, blood dripping from every orifice.

"Fuck! The gas!" Foster shouts.

More techs fall, their bodies being dissolved from the inside out. But others finally find their feet, turn and bolt to a sealed Plexiglas door at the far end of the room. Alpha Team beats them to it.

"Key this open, now!" Foster orders one of the techs. The man, hands shaking, barely gets the code in before his eyes roll up into his head, the whites now a dark red as the capillaries burst.

She pushes the body out of the way and moves forward as her Team starts shoving techs through the door behind her. She is in a long, steel-walled corridor, her rifle to her shoulder as she walks carefully towards an airlock at the opposite end. Zorn tells the techs that haven't died to shut the fuck up, but no one listens. Foster ignores the chaos, knowing her people have her back, and focuses only on the airlock. The wheel in the center begins to spin and she stops, takes a knee, and prepares to fire.

"Hold," Joe T says over the com as the airlock swings wide. "It's me."

The size of a small mountain, Joe T's deep chocolate skinned face smiles behind his mask as he nods to Foster.

"Didn't have to take a knee for me, boss," Joe T says. "A simple curtsey would have done."

"Fuck you," Foster says as she gets up. "You find them?"

"I think so," Joe T says. "But it won't be easy."

Foster follows him as he turns and starts to jog back to his Team. She does a quick head count and sees that he's only at half strength.

"You got hit hard," she states.

"No shit," Joe T responds. "Some of the security guards can shoot. The ones that couldn't set off charges." He points to a large vault door. "I'm guessing we go in there."

Music fills the air around them to the tune of "Wheels On The Bus," but with very different words.

"We kill the soldiers because they hate us, they hate us, they hate us," the song echoes everywhere. "We kill the soldiers because they hate us, they all must die."

Men behind Foster start to scream and the com is filled with cries of pain and surprise.

"What the fuck?" Foster says as she spins about to see the techs left alive going completely berserk on her men.

Masks are ripped off and fingers go straight for eyes. Teeth find flesh and rip. Men fall as they are pounced on from people that had been docile just seconds before, but are now raging, homicidal maniacs.

"Drop them!" Foster shouts and the firing begins.

With surgical precision, every tech is put down. Most have perfectly spaced holes in their backs, while some are missing most of their heads. Either way they are all killed quickly.

"Sound off!" Foster orders as she ejects her spent magazine and slams in a fresh one. After the roll call, she realizes they are down to less than half strength. Fuck.

Then the wheel in the center of the vault door starts to turn. All rifles take aim as the messed up children's song keeps playing over and over. But the sound changes. It no longer comes from the speakers, but from behind the vault door as the massive hunk of steel swings open.

Standing before the armed contractors are twelve teenage women. Blondes, brunettes, redheads, all dressed in dark grey tank tops with skintight black pants tucked into black combat boots. In each hand, they hold long blades that look dangerously sharp.

They are the voices singing now, taking over for the voice in the speakers.

"We kill the soldiers because they hate us, they hate us, they hate us," they all sing. "We kill the soldiers because they hate us. And it's fun to watch them die!"

The speed.

When it is all over that is one thing Foster remembers until her last breath, the speed.

She was born into the military life, has seen combat on every single continent across the globe, but has never seen speed like that before. The girls move like cranked up cats, the blades out like claws, their arms swinging this way and that, leaving nothing but blood and screams in their wake.

Foster ducks a blade and jams her rifle into the solar plexus of the redhead that tries to kill her. The girl grunts and staggers, unable to overcome the hit. Foster doesn't hesitate, knowing a thing

"Not the objective," Foster responds as she pulls several zip ties from her pocket. She leans over a girl, flips her onto her stomach and ties her wrists together then her ankles. "I doubt the esteemed Doctor Kramer stuck around to watch the show. He's probably long gone by now."

The Team is able to get the girls secured and hurry to haul the sleeping bodies outside to a wide clearing. Rifles at the shoulders, the Team watches the tree line around them and the ridges above, never taking their safety for granted.

"Come on," Foster whispers. "Where the fuck are you?"

***

"Ma'am!" the chopper pilot shouts as he steps from the helicopter. "Ma'am! You need to move!"

The pilot watches as a woman staggers towards him, her body covered in only a torn nightgown despite the chill in the early morning air. A grunt and a moan draws his attention to the trees beyond and he sees a man dressed in only boxers come stumbling out from behind a large oak.

"Fucking hillbillies."

The woman opens her mouth and hisses at the pilot, sending cold chills up and down his spine. He slowly draws the pistol from his belt, holding it firmly down and against his leg.

"Ma'am, I don't know what drugs you are on, but you need to step away from my bird," the pilot yells.

"Dell? This is Bedford," a voice says over the com. "Why aren't you in the air?"

"A problem with the locals," Dell replies. "It's getting a little Deliverance here."

"I don't care. I have my own shit to deal with. Things are fucking weird," Bedford says. "Get to the LZ and extract Foster's Team now."

"Roger," Dell says and holsters his pistol. "See if I care if this bitch gets chopped to bits."

Dell hops back in the chopper and slams his door shut. The woman keeps coming at him, but he just flips her off and starts to prepare for takeoff. Just as he is about to lift up, the woman reaches the chopper and starts banging on the door, making Dell jump.

"Jesus!" he yells. "What the fuck is...wrong...with... Holy *shit*..."

The woman's face is smeared with blood and bits of flesh hang from her mouth. She snarls at Dell and slams her forehead against the chopper while her hands, also covered in blood, slap against the Plexiglas.

"Command?" Dell calls over the com, looking past the woman to the man. He has friends.

"What is it, Dell?" Bedford asks. "I don't have time for this."

"When you said things are getting weird, what did you mean?" Dell asks. "Did you mean like crazy people covered in *blood* weird?"

"It looks like that," Bedford says. "We don't have all the intel yet."

Dawn light crests over the ridge of the cove the chopper is tucked away in, lighting up the man and his friends. Like the woman, they are all covered in blood. One of them is carrying what looks like a doll's arm. But as Dell watches blood drip from the end, he quickly thinks it didn't ever belong to a doll.

He knows for certain when the woman carrying the arm jams it into her mouth and starts chewing.

"Holy fuck," Dell says. "I'm getting the fuck out of here."

He starts to lift the chopper, but it tilts wildly, unbalanced on one side. Dell looks over and sees that a whole crowd has snuck up on him while he was busy watching the woman and the people behind her. A blood covered, gore smeared mob has the skids pinned as they surround the chopper. Dell thinks he can get some lift and maybe shake them off, so he pulls up on the stick.

He's wrong.

Everything goes to shit fast and the chopper begins to spin wildly. The rear rotor slams into the part of the mob that aren't caught in the skids, spraying the landscape with blood. Dell tries not to puke as guts splatter the windshield. He fails.

The tail catches on a short pine and the chopper tips, sending the main rotor into the ground. The blades snap in half as the helicopter spins and falls to its side. Stunned, covered in his own sick, and terrified by the insanity about him, Dell pulls his pistol, kicks the side door open, and hauls himself up out of the smoking chopper.

The area around him is covered in blood. But that doesn't stop any of the people from stepping right through it on their way to him.

"What the fuck is wrong with you fucks?" Dell shouts as he empties his pistol into the mob. He sees the slugs rip open chests and hit legs and he watches the people fall. Then he watches them get back up. He keeps pulling the trigger, the sound of the empty pistol echoing along with the moans and groans of the mob.

Dell fumbles at his belt, trying desperately to find the extra magazines for his pistol. His hand finds one just as a hand grips his ankle. He screams and looks down. Below him is the first woman. Or half of her at least. The bottom half is gone and all that is left are intestines hanging from her torso.

"Holy fuck!" Dell screams as the woman starts to climb his body.

He ejects his spent magazine, tries to get the fresh one in, but fumbles it. It falls and smacks the woman right between the eyes. She hisses then opens her mouth wide and chomps down onto his leg. Dell screams as he feels her teeth tear into his flesh, going right through the pants leg.

He pulls his arm back, ready to punch her in the face and knock her off him, but his arm is caught. Dell looks over his shoulder and the blood drains from his face as the piss drains from his bladder. The last thing he sees is a mouth of bloody teeth.

***

"Command!" Foster yells. "Where the fuck is the chopper?"

"No go, Foster," Bedford replies. "We lost contact with Dell. Secure yourself and the cargo. It could be a while before we can get you out of there."

"What the fuck are you talking about?" Foster yells. "I am going to have your ass for this, Bedford!"

"I know, boss," Bedford replies. "But we have- HOLY FUCK!"

The com goes dead leaving a slight ringing and a hiss of static in Foster's ear.

"Command? Command? Bedford, do you read me?" Foster calls. "Bedford! What the fuck is going on there?"

There is no reply.

"Uh, boss?" Zorn says. "We have company."

Foster turns her attention back to the facility and frowns. "I thought we terminated the staff."

"We did," Zorn replies. "After they went all ape shit we put them all down."

"Some got back up," Joe T replies. "Jesus, I killed that guy myself. Look at the placement on his chest."

A couple dozen staff members, moaning and groaning, shamble their way towards the Team. Most of them are covered in blood from the chest wounds they received when they were shot. It doesn't even faze them.

"Boss? Orders?" Zorn asks.

"Take 'em out," Foster replies as she opens fire.

The staff begin to shudder and shake like a grotesque, country line dance. Then they fall. The Team all wait, their rifles still up. Every one of them have their senses set to high, their guts telling them it isn't over. And it isn't.

One by one, the staff begins to rise.

"Not possible," one of the Team members says. "Not fucking possible."

"Don't say something isn't possible when you are watching it happen," Foster snaps. "Head shots. Now."

The rifles bark and brains fly. The staff drops again. The Team waits. This time they don't get back up. The Team keeps waiting. Still no movement.

"I've seen this movie," Joe T says, "it doesn't end well."

"I want a supply check now!" Foster orders. "We are on our own until we hear from Command."

The Team takes stock of their ammunition and supplies. No one is pleased.

"Orders, boss?" Zorn asks Foster.

She starts to answer but is interrupted by one of the girls on the ground.

"Not with the way the roads are," Bedford says. "Every major interstate is clogged. Takes forever to clear room. They are using back highways and side roads. I'll send you exact extraction coordinates when they get closer. For now just do whatever you are doing to stay alive."

"Roger that," Foster says, "and hey, Bedford?"

"Yeah, boss?"

"It's good to hear your voice," Foster says.

"You too, boss."

***

"Brittany just ate my ass!" a girl yells, her arms up in the air as she stands over the slumped form at her feet. "Game, set, and match, beeyotch!"

"That's enough, Carly," Foster says as she walks into the workout room. "I need everyone's attention."

"Yes, Ms. Foster!" twelve teenage girls say in unison as they all step in line, even the one from the floor who is busy rubbing the bruise that is quickly forming on her right cheek.

"What's up, boss?" Zorn says from the side of the room just before he pops a cracker with peanut butter into his mouth. "We gugga go hone nah?"

"Yes," Foster says.

This gets Zorn's attention quickly, as well as the attention of the few other men that are busy lounging against the walls of the workout room. "Where's Joe T?"

"Killing zeds," a Team member answers. "A horde just showed up outside. He's with Cooper and LeRoy clearing them out."

"Good," Foster says. "We are all going to go help. Time you girls learned how to handle the new world. I have two days to get you ready so that we get out of here alive."

One of the girls pulls a large knife and flips it around the back of her hand before tossing it across the room where it sticks in the wall right between the heads of two Team members. "Not a problem."

The two Team members close on the girl, pissed at her little stunt, but she is quickly surrounded by the rest of the girls. The men back off without hesitation.

Foster can't help but smile.

"That's my girls," she says. "What's our motto?"

They all start singing the nursery rhyme, but with newer words. "The world can suck my big fat dick, big fat dick, big fat dick," they sing in unison. "The world can suck my big fat dick 'cause the dead ain't gonna get us!"

"Fucking A right," Foster nods. "Now let's help Joe T kill some zeds. Watch your backs, watch your sisters' backs, watch my back."

"Yes, Ms. Foster," they all say as they sprint for the door.

***

Z-Day plus thirty-two.

Foster kneels by the side of the road, hidden in a thicket of rhododendrons. Behind her, concealed by the dense foliage are the rest of her Team and her girls.

Her girls.

That's how she has come to think of them over the past thirty-two days. Once she realized how suggestible they were, she took advantage quick and made them hers. Unless someone with a will stronger than hers comes along, she has twelve girls ready to kill or die for her. A handy thing to have in the zombie apocalypse.

She has a hard time coming to terms with the whole idea of the dead coming back and walking the Earth, but that's the reality of things. The world is in ruins and she has no intention of going down with it. All she has to do is get her girls into the Humvees then keep them safe during the travel back to headquarters.

Not that they can't take care of themselves.

Whatever Kramer had planned for them, it included combat. All Foster had to do was add some discipline and focus to their conditioning and she had an instant fighting unit ready to do whatever she wanted. For a person like Foster it was side by side with winning the lottery.

"Engines," Joe T says as he nods to the north and a bend in the road. "Here we go."

Within seconds, a convoy of six Humvees come into view, each with a manned .50 caliber machine gun on top. Foster stands and moves to the side of the road and the convoy comes to a stop next to her. None of the men manning the guns even glance her way, their eyes locked on the surroundings, watching, waiting, careful.

"Hey, boss," a woman smiles from the driver's seat, "you're a damn good sight to see."

"Torres," Foster nods. She turns and gives a low whistle. The Team and the girls all hustle from their concealment and load up into the Humvees. It takes less than five seconds. Foster hops into the passenger seat of the lead Humvee and nods. "Get us the fuck out of here, Lourdes."

"On it," Lourdes says, "but we'll have to circle around Asheville. We drew a herd with us as we came down from Weaverville. They were just hanging out on one of the roads, like they were having a fucking block party or something."

"How many?" Foster asks.

"Couple hundred," Lourdes says as she puts the Humvee into gear and hits the gas. "We got by fine, but no way we can backtrack directly."

"Fine," Foster says, "just drive. We'll get around them."

The convoy drives.

They spend an hour trying to get turned around. The GPS in the Humvees still work thanks to the magic of satellites, but the little black boxes can't show them where the zeds are. Or what roads are blocked with debris. There is a surprising amount of debris crossing the roads.

"This isn't right," Foster says, "this feels deliberate."

"My gut has the same feeling," Lourdes nods. "What's the call?"

A bridge lies ahead and the convoy starts to cross it. Foster's Humvee is the first across and comes around an immediate turn in the road. Lourdes slams on the brakes to avoid ramming into an eighteen wheeler that is parked lengthwise, blocking them.

"Get ready!" Foster shouts into the com. She barely has the words out before gunfire erupts everywhere. "Fuck!"

"Fucking ambush!" Lourdes yells as she grabs her rifle and shoves the door open.

She sprints towards the side of the road and dives into the brush just as a man comes out, a double-barrel shotgun in hand. She rolls and comes up fast, her fist nailing him in the balls. He grunts then is dropped as she sweeps his legs. Quickly relieved of his shotgun, he finds the barrels pressed up against his chin.

"Idiot," Lourdes says as she pulls the triggers, turning the top of his head into a grey matter and blood fountain.

"Return fire!" Foster yells as she jumps from the Humvee. "Find cover!"

But there's no cover for the five Humvees on the bridge; they are sitting ducks. The .50 calibers open up, firing indiscriminately, but soon go quiet as one by one the men behind them are taken out. It was something Foster was worried about. Sport hunters in the apocalypse. They can't fight, but they can shoot. The Humvees, and everyone in them, are sitting ducks.

"Girls!" Foster screams into the com. "Girls! JUMP!"

"But, Ms. Foster," one of them replies.

"Don't fucking argue!" Foster snaps as she puts a bullet between the eyes of a man running at her. With an axe. Really? Moron. She watches him fall and her mind takes in his appearance: dirt covered, torn clothes, emaciated. Survivors. Scavengers. The dregs of the apocalypse.

Only took thirty days to go completely to shit.

The girls don't argue and the Humvee doors fly open. Foster turns just in time to see the twelve girls briefly hesitate then leap from the bridge into the churning waters below. She can't watch long as she feels a bullet burn past her cheek. She spins and drops the offender.

The fight lasts for another fifteen minutes before voices come over the com.

"Clear!" Joe T shouts.

"Clear!" yells Zorn.

"Clear!" Lourdes adds, as do a handful of other voices. Much less than what they started with.

Z-Day plus three hundred fifty-five.

"They killed him, Pa!" Elsbeth cries as she runs along the French Broad River. "They shot Uncle Jeb right in the eyehole!" Her face is scrunched up with rage. "I'll kill all them! All them!"

"Shut it, girlie," Pa snarls as he tries to keep up. He coughs and shivers at the pain in his chest and face. Reaching up, he worries at the hole in his right cheek and a hole that keeps getting bigger and bigger, smelling of rot and puss. "You'll bring the dead down on us."

Elsbeth looks around, her eyes scanning the woods. She shuts it. Doesn't want to anger Pa. Not while he's sick. Not while the green stuff keeps eating his face.

They don't stop running until they hit I-26. Then they see the horde of Zs that shamble and shuffle between the wrecked cars that litter the interstate. Elsbeth ducks low, as does Pa and they crouch by the side of the road, waiting for their chance. After a few minutes, they see an opportunity and sprint across, scrambling up the hillside and back into the cover of trees.

A few Zs turn and start to follow, but they can't get purchase on the loose soil. They stop after a few minutes and join their fellow undead, going back to the familiar artery of lives they can't remember.

***

Z-Day plus three hundred seventy.

"What do we do now, Pa?" Elsbeth asks, huddled into the corner of the basement, a damp tarp wrapped around her to fight off the cold as Pa tries to get a fire going. "None of the houses have no foods left. We picked 'em clean. No foods up in the woods, had to leave. No foods down here in the city. That mean we haves ta leave too?"

"Quiet," Pa hisses.

"But I's just..."

"Quiet!" Pa snaps. "Listen!"

She quiets and hears what he hears. Screaming.

"Some woman needs help up there," Elsbeth says.

"She does," Pa says. Then smiles.

The smile. The smile. The smile.

Elsbeth shudders.

"Let's go help her," Pa says.

They do.

They fight off the Zs that have the woman and her wounded husband surrounded. They help her carry him back to their basement. They help her have a seat on the floor by the fire. They help her watch as Pa bashes her husband's brains out. They help her with her grief by bashing her brains out.

Then they help themselves.

To her.

"Huh? I didn't say anything," I reply.

"You have been acting like you need to pee," Elsbeth says. "That means you want to say something. Most people it means they need to pee. Not Long Pork." She shakes her head. "Means he has something to say, but is too much of a pussy to say it."

"Well, now that you've buttered me up, I guess I'll spill it," I say.

"I didn't put butter on you," she frowns. "I don't eat people anymore. Why are you being so mean?"

"Whoa, whoa, it's just an expression."

"Stupid expression."

"Yeah, I guess it is," I say. "Wonder where it came from? Who was the first person to decide that you should put butter on someone? What the hell is that..."

"Long Pork!" Elsbeth shouts.

I can hear a few hammers close by stop. People get twitchy when Elsbeth shouts. Not without reason. She is one badass cannibal savant even if she has given up her taste for thigh meat.

"Sorry," I say. I set the hammer down by the stack of fence boards. "I do have something to say." The impatient way she looks at me hurries my ass up. I think she's actually ready to pop me one. "You've been going off on your own a lot lately. Just wondering what's up. In fact, I'm not the only one wondering."

"I'm looking for cannies, like you all want," Elsbeth says quickly. She had that one planned. I don't buy it.

"We've cleared out all of North Asheville as well as downtown," I say. "There are still random survivors in West Asheville, as well as out in East Asheville. But you're going south."

Elsbeth just stares.

"And I think Lourdes and her people have South Asheville covered," I continue. "They've said so. So, still wondering where you're going."

"How do you know I'm going south?" Elsbeth asks, her head tilting to the side. You know, like a curious lioness just before she pounces on some poor, wounded animal.

"Um, well... I guessed?"

"You're a bad liar, Long Pork."

28

"So are you."

Ooooh, she doesn't like that.

"Who says I'm lying? I'm looking for cannies. That's what I said. It's true."

It's my turn to give her a "look." It isn't anywhere close to as effective as her look.

"Where are you really going, El?" I ask bluntly. No time for the Jace and Elsbeth dance. I'm tired.

Her face scrunches up and I tense my entire body, not sure where she's going to hit me. Then she relaxes and sits down on the stack of fence boards. They shift and slide out from under her and she falls on her ass. Before I can even think to laugh at the slapstick, she shoots me a death glare that takes about eight years off my life expectancy.

I do not laugh. No laughing.

Once she has her embarrass rage under control, she shakes her head and sighs.

"I'm following the girls," she says.

I have a feeling she expects me to know what this means.

"Not following you," I say.

"Yes, they are," she replies.

Shit. Now I'm really lost. I grab a seat next to her.

"Start over," I say. "What the fuck is going on?"

"The girls that have been following me and watching us," Elsbeth says, her voice intoning that I'm a complete moron. "I follow them. They don't know."

Too many questions go through my head.

"Okay, we'll get to the 'watching us' part later," I say. "Where do you follow them to?"

"That big house," she says, "with all the fields and woods around it."

"Going to have to narrow it down for me," I say. "That describes a shit ton of houses around Asheville. Every douchebag that had Biltmore envy built one of those."

"Yes, that place," she smiles. "You're smart, Long Pork." She punches me on the shoulder. My confusion is what distracts me from the pain.

"El, I love you like family..."

Stella. My wife. Board Chairperson for the Whispering Pines Homeowners' association. As leader of the HOA she is supposed to go to the Grove Park and meet with Lourdes Torres (commander of the private military contractors), Ed Lassiter (leader of the Labor Force), Big Daddy Fitzpatrick (head of the Farm), and Critter (Big Daddy's brother and leader of whatever the fuck he's leader of). It's the monthly Survivor Counsel meeting.

"Why does she need me?" Elsbeth asks.

We find out quickly as we walk into my house, one of the very first that was rebuilt from the many scraps and components of the abandoned neighborhoods around us.

"Hey, baby," Stella says from the couch, "I'm sick. It was the apples."

"I told you they were too green," I say.

"But they tasted so good," she sighs. "Can you go in my place today?"

"Sure," I say, "I'll get cleaned up. What'd you need Elsbeth for?"

"She's going with you," Stella says.

"I can take care of myself," I snap.

"Yes, yes you can," Stella sighs, "but I'd feel better if she was with you. Okay?"

"Oooh," Elsbeth smiles. "I can go swimming!" She claps her hands and does a little dance.

"Can I go?" Greta, our fourteen year old daughter asks from the walkway above. "I want to go swimming. And Tansy and Becka will be there."

"Not today, sweetie," Stella says. "You and your brother have chores. The house needs to be cleaned."

"Seriously? That's bullshit," Greta snaps. "We're always cleaning the house! What do you do? Just sit on the couch and..."

"I'd stop there," I say, seeing the look on my wife's face. "Greta? Go get your brother and start cleaning."

"It's like ninety degrees in here!" she shouts. "I'll die!"

"Then you'll come back as a Z and I'll kill you," Elsbeth says. Silence.

"I'll get Charlie," Greta says and tucks away quickly.

"Thanks, El," Stella says, "she needed a swift kick like that."

"What?" Elsbeth asks. "I didn't say I'd kick her, I said I'd kill her."

"Right," Stella smiles, "whatever, it worked. Jace?"

"Getting clean then we are out of here," I say, leaning over the couch and kissing her. "Love you."

"Love you too."

***

Melissa Billings, our head of the scavenging crew, drives the four door pickup truck as we wind up Elk Mountain Road on our way to the Grove Park. I sit up front with her while Elsbeth sits in the back seat and her eyes watching the empty houses zip by. The truck bed is filled with heavily armed men and women, part of Lourdes's crew. They accompany everyone everywhere. It's greatly reduced the casualty rate that can get kinda high in the zombie apocalypse.

Melissa keeps glancing at me out of the corner of her eye and it's really bugging the shit out of me.

"What?" I ask. "Out with it."

"We have to make a detour," she says. "Need to pick someone up."

"Pick someone up? Who? There's nothing between here and the Grove Park except... No. No fucking way." I shake my head like a three year old having a tantrum. "No, no, no. I'll kill the bitch."

After my shower, I switched up my prosthetic and put on my "in the field" arm. It's a long spike, deadly sharp at the end. Mr. Spikey. If we get in the shit then I'm ready to brain some Zs. It's not an easy thing to do, but I've gotten pretty good with it. I hold up Mr. Spikey and wave it by Melissa's face.

"I. Will. Stab. Her," I say.

Elsbeth snickers from the back seat. I turn on her, pissed. She glares. I turn back, not quite as pissed.

"They are putting the last touches on their fortifications," Melissa says, ignoring my hissy fit. "She can get away for the meeting, but can't spare any of her people."

"Her people?" I snort. "Fucking dipshits."

Brenda Kelly, the former Chairperson of the Whispering Pines HOA. Stella took her job. It was a bloodless coup, done all democratic like and all.

But that woman…

She's a squat, ugly, goblin-beast of a bitch. The woman is pure evil, in my honest opinion. She colluded with Vance, but still got reelected because of fear and stupidity. It wasn't until Stella stepped up and took over that she lost her power base. But, being an evil twat, she quickly found a new power base.

The laborers. The slaves that were brought to Asheville by Anthony Mondello (I refuse to call him the POTUS) and Ms. Foster (Lourdes's former boss) to rebuild and secure the Blue Ridge Parkway.

Most of the laborers decided to stick around and stay at the Grove Park Inn. The problem is that so did the private military contractors, or PCs that had been their guards and captors. Tension is an understatement. And Brenda Kelly (did I mention the evil twat part?) grabbed onto that tension and pulled hard.

She quickly got a faction of laborers to back her and make a move to take over Reynolds Mountain. Years before Z-day, Reynolds Mountain was a planned development in Woodfin/North Asheville. A mix of "upscale" shops and cafes at the base with a luxury, private neighborhood overlooking it from the mountain above. They have spent the past few months fortifying the development, keeping the Zs at bay. It's like a version of Whispering Pines, but with marble countertops and bidets.

"You're just pissed because you didn't think of it," Melissa says, echoing my thoughts perfectly.

She's right. I am pissed. I want marble countertops. I could do without the bidets. Never could figure that shit out. I mean, what do you do afterwards? Drip dry? It's all so confusing!

"Am not," I lie.

"Get over it, Jace," Melissa says. "Is she an evil twat? Yes." Ha! Told ya! "But she has a right to be a part of Asheville, just like all of us. As long as she doesn't try anything."

"And that's the real problem," I snap. "Eventually she will try something. That's what evil twats do!"

"They also stink," Elsbeth says.

"What?" I ask.

She waves her hand in front of her nose. "Evil twats stink. Smelly pussy."

Melissa tries to keep it under control, but she bursts out laughing. I shake my head and smile then start laughing too.

"What?" Elsbeth frowns. "Don't laugh at me? You laugh at me too much."

"No, no, darling," Melissa says, "I'm not laughing at you. You just crack me up sometimes, okay? That's a good thing."

Elsbeth smiles. "Okay. Good."

Mood swings don't even begin to describe the woman sitting behind me...

We cross over I-26 and I look down at the interstate below. The Zs are back. For a while, they had been cleared out by Vance, corralled into a massive pen he made out of draining Beaver Lake. We killed those after I took Vance down. But, Zs have some semblance of the habits of their old lives and always congregate in places they may have frequented when alive. It didn't take long before other Zs made their way to their asphalt altar. Says a lot about our former commuter society, doesn't it?

Instead of going straight onto Lakeshore Drive, Melissa turns left onto Woodfin Ave, heading to Reynolds Mountain. My gut clenches, as do my fists, but I keep it under control. Kinda have to with the gut clench or I'll shit myself. That's never fun. Trust me.

We have to cross Merrimon Ave and then drive through the old Reynolds Village. I used to go to the YMCA there. What? I went there. Twice. Shut up.

The road twists through a thick woods of pine before we come to a massive set of wooden gates. Huh, wonder where she got that design from? Gate design stealing twat.

Up, up, up we go. Some residents wave at us, recognizing Melissa's truck. Some just stare, not trusting anyone that isn't a direct neighbor. More than a few flip us off. Okay, they flip me off. I'm not exactly a favorite in these here parts.

I don't even acknowledge the woman when we pull up to the fucking mansion she's taken as her home. I guess she does share it with her right hand, Mindy Sterling, who used to be the Head of Security for Whispering Pines. Elsbeth's manfriend, Julio, has taken that duty since Mindy decided to keep her nose wedged up her boss's ass.

"Hey, Jace," Mindy says to me then shuts up as she gets a death glare from Brenda.

The two women pull their collective bulks into the back with Elsbeth. Melissa just nods at them then pulls away.

"What do you think of our fortifications, Mr. Stanford?" Brenda asks as the massive gate closes behind us, shutting the development off from the rest of the Z infested world. "I'm sure it's not up to your brilliant standards, but we haven't had a breach yet."

I grunt.

"I'll take that as a compliment," Brenda sneers. Not that I see the sneer since I'm focusing on the road in front of us and refuse to turn and look at her. But I hear that sneer. That snippy, smarmy sneer...

We pull out onto Merrimon Ave and drive south towards the Grove Park. Everyone sits in silence. Mindy tries to make conversation, but every time she opens her mouth, Elsbeth turns to her and frowns. She shuts up.

Our phones chime. All of our phones. Landon has been busy making sure the Wi-Fi is city wide. Solar batteries and routers everywhere.

"LAKE JULIAN UNDER SIEGE! ALL HANDS NOW!"

"Fuck," I say. The power plant.

Albert Shumway, a muscled fireplug that works under Lourdes's supervision has spent months retrofitting the Lake Julian power plant from coal into natural gas, which luckily we are flush with in Asheville. He's an ornery asshole and we haven't gotten along well, but he does know his power plants. He's made a lot of progress with getting us closer to city wide power.

If the Zs would leave the plant the fuck alone.

For some reason, and none of us can figure out what it is, the Zs like the power plant. They migrate there in hordes. Thirty, forty, fifty at a time they show up. Half the week is spent killing Zs and not working on the plant.

It sounds like there's more of a herd this time than a horde.

"Status?" I text back.

"FUCK YOUR STATUS, STANFORD! I NEED EVERYONE HERE NOW! FUCKING HERD!"

I was right. Not that I want to be right about this. I like being right in Trivial Pursuit, not about civilization-crushing Z herds.

"Looks like the meeting is postponed," Melissa says as she floors it.

"What?" Brenda screeches (it's her default tone). "You aren't dropping us at the Grove Park?"

Melissa hooks a thumb at the men and women in the bed of the truck. "Everyone means everyone, Brenda. It doesn't mean make a pit stop to let you out so you can lounge by the pool."

"Oh," Mindy says. I guess she had planned on lounging by the pool.

"Well, don't expect me to fight," Brenda says. "I'm a leader, not a fighter."

"You're a slug," Elsbeth says.

Brenda starts to reply then realizes who she is replying to and shuts the fuck up right quick.

"You know where Stuart is?" Melissa asks.

"Nope," I say. "I'll try to find out. We'll need him."

"He's with Julio," Elsbeth says.

"He is?" I ask. "How do you know?"

I look over my shoulder and she just stares at me.

***

When Z-Day hit it was a Sunday.

The day is only significant because on the Biltmore Estate, that's a busy day. Thousands of tourists crowded the sprawling house, and surrounding grounds of one of America's former families of robber baron royalty. The Vanderbilts.

For some inexplicable reason, the management of the estate decided to lock down everything when the dead began to rise. They closed and barred the gates, barricaded access roads, fenced off bridges. There was no way in or out.

Did they get a heads up? Did someone say, "Hey, zombie apocalypse! Everyone's sleeping here tonight!"

No one knows because within days the place was nothing but a nest of Zs.

Odds are someone had a heart attack and it all went downhill from there. One guy gets up a little peckish for human flesh and pretty soon it's the meme of the day to eat your friends, family, fellow flabby tourists.

Whatever the circumstances, the Biltmore Estate pretty much stayed off limits to the survivors of Asheville. Why would anyone even bother when faced with a sea of undead shambling around the grounds? And there is a sea of them. Thousands standing in the fields, their moans and groans, hisses and snarls echoing about the landscape. They just stand there. Waiting…

"What are they waiting for?" Julio asks as he lowers his binoculars. "They don't leave the estate. Just hang out in the fields."

His companion grunts, but doesn't lower his binoculars.

"I don't think they can move," Stuart says.

"Come again?" Julio asks.

The two men are perched on a hill that overlooks the estate. They have a good view of the many fields and gardens that once grew corn and wheat, pastured beef and dairy cows, and each season flourished with a multitude of wildflowers.

"They move," Julio says.

"No, they don't," Stuart says. "They move their arms, and some move a leg back and forth, but none of them actually leave where they are standing." He lowers his binoculars and rubs at the bridge of his nose. "It's like they are glued into place."

Julio has another look and frowns. "Yeah, I guess you're right. I never noticed that. I assumed they were just doing that Z thing where they stare at shit until some asshole comes along and gets them worked up."

"That's not an accident," Stuart says, "someone put them there."

"Nah, man, they were already there," Julio says, studying the tattered and shredded clothing that still dangles from many of the Zs.

Wearing remnants of their former lives, they are covered in t-shirts with logos from their favorite bands, sports teams, universities, bulky sweatshirts with majestic eagles, grizzly bears, monster trucks, couture and faux couture blouses and jeans.

A slice of 21st century fashion pre-Z.

"I mean that someone placed them where they stand," Stuart says. "Moved them from where they were wandering about the estate and into their current positions."

"And why the fuck would someone do that?" Julio asks.

"Keeps us from going in there," Stuart says. "Even keeps Critter and his crew from scavenging the place. If Critter won't touch it then no one will."

"True dat," Julio says. "So now what?"

"I don't know," Stuart says. "Why does Elsbeth keep coming here then? Has she gone inside yet and we don't know? What is drawing her to an estate with a staged herd of Zs?"

"All good questions, man," Julio replies. "Let me know when you have answers."

He watches for a second then pulls the binoculars away. Then puts them back. Then away.

"There's someone down in that shit," Julio says. "Take a look, man. Someone is moving through those fuckers."

"Probably just a Z that got loose," Stuart says as he starts scanning the field. "Where am I looking then?"

"About thirty yards in from the left," Julio says, "second field back."

"I got it," Stuart says, "is that a girl? A woman? Can't tell. Fucker is hiding behind a Z."

"Ballsy," Julio says. "Lucky she doesn't get her tits bitten off."

"Nice," Stuart frowns. "Maybe a survivor that wandered onto the grounds. Now trying to get out."

"You believe that?" Julio asks.

"No," Stuart replies. Their phones vibrate. "Check that."

"Why don't you check yours?" Julio asks.

"Seriously?" Stuart replies. One word, one question, no room for argument.

"Fine," Julio says as he pulls his phone out of his pocket. "Surprised Landon got Wi-Fi to reach this far."

"The guy may be an asshole, but he does stay focused when given a task," Stuart says.

"Still a total asshole though," Julio replies as he reads the message. "Ah, shit, man, we gotta go."

"What is it then?" Stuart asks, looking at Julio.

"Power plant is under attack," Julio replies. "We picked the wrong day to go for a hike. Maybe we can find a car that still runs and hotwire the bitch. Drive it down to help out?"

Their phones buzz again.

"Never mind," Julio smiles. "It's Jace wondering where we are. He's with Mel and they are on their way."

He taps at the virtual keyboard and sends his response.

"What's the plan?" Stuart asks.

"We'll meet them on Hendersonville Rd," Julio says. "They'll give us a ride down to Lake Julian."

"Huh," Stuart says and looks at Julio dressed in only jeans and a black tank top. "Not really outfitted for combat."

"Neither are you," Julio says, nodding at Stuart's almost identical outfit except he's wearing a black t-shirt instead of a tank. "But Shumway'll have supplies."

"He does," Stuart nods as he crawls backwards from their vantage point, not wanting to be seen standing up by whomever is in the field. Or whomever else could be in the area, watching.

***

The flashes of light, obvious reflections from binoculars, stop and a young woman waits, her eyes watching the hilltop closely. She doesn't see any other signs of movement and figures the spies have gone away. But she doesn't move for another thirty minutes just to be sure. The Z she crouches behind groans and reaches for her face, as it has done for the past hour.

"Stop," she whispers, swatting the rotten hand away. "No more, Cecil."

The Z doesn't understand the words, just the hunger that torments it day and night. Having food, sweet, living flesh so close would have sent any other Z into a frenzy, but this Z, Cecil apparently, hasn't eaten in years. It's emaciated and weak and barely has the strength to curl its fingers into a fist. With grey, starving eyes it watches the young woman scramble away, lost in the herd of its undead brethren.

"See ya later, Cecil," the young woman whispers. "Stay cool."

***

Melissa barely slows the truck for Stuart and Julio.

"Hop in back," I say as we roll up to the two men. "Crowded in here."

"Special guests?" Stuart asks as he grabs the side of the truck and vaults into the bed as the PCs make room.

Elsbeth slides the back window open and smiles as Julio joins everyone else.

"Hey there," she says. "Can we do it tonight?"

"Jesus," Julio says and shakes his head as the PCs chuckle around him.

"That is highly inappropriate," Brenda snips.

"Oh, you're here," Stuart says, looking into the cab and seeing the former head of Whispering Pines. "Plan to get your hands dirty this time?"

"I will do no such thing," Brenda snaps. "You can do the fighting. That's what you know. I know how to lead, despite some other people's opinions."

"By 'other people' she means anyone with some semblance of sanity left in their heads," I say.

"Yeah, I get that one," Stuart replies. "Thanks for clearing that up, Jace."

"It is unbelievably rude to criticize a head of state like that," Brenda says. "Your diplomacy skills are sorely lacking."

"Head of state?" I snort. "Are you fucking kidding me?"

I turn around and finally look at the woman.

"You are the head of nothing, bitch," I snarl. "What you are is a backstabbing, self-serving, scum-sucking, blob of useless fat that needs to be wiped off this planet before there is any chance of your kind multiplying by asexual fragmentation!" I take a deep breath. "Bitch."

"Asexual fragmentation?" Stuart asks. "Wow. You're really riled up today."

"I will report this behavior to the Counsel, you know," Brenda says. "Whether you like me or not you do have to respect my position amongst the survivors, Mr. Stanford!"

"I don't have to respect shit, you fucking whore-ass cunt!" I shout.

Then I lunge over the back of the seat at her. I just can't take the woman anymore. All I want to do is grab her and shove her out the fucking door. Let her roll down the road and hope a horde comes by and eats her fat ass.

"Jace!"

"Long Pork!"

"Damn, dude!"

"God dammit, Stanford," Stuart yells as he reaches in and slaps me before I can throttle the evil twat. "Get a hold of yourself! We'd all like to see the woman dead, but we are rebuilding a society, not destroying one. Calm the fuck down!"

I do calm down and Melissa grabs me by the scruff of my shirt and yanks me all the way into my seat. Which causes her to swerve to the side and slam into a Z that's just decided to step out into the road. It reaches for us and then it's gone, lost under the truck.

The vehicle gives a shudder and bounce and some blood and gunk spray out from underneath. We get about fifteen yards before we feel the trouble.

"That's a flat," Melissa growls, looking over at me, her eyes all accusatory and shit. "Because we hit a Z."

"Should have watched the road," I say, knowing it's not fair or even nice. But I'm pissed.

She pulls the truck over and the PCs jump out to create a perimeter, their rifles to their shoulders. Melissa leans over me and opens my door.

"This is your job, Jason," she says. "Better hurry. Anyone dies because we got held up and it's on your head."

"Sure, make the one armed man do it," I mutter as I get out.

The back right tire is dead flat. The Z must have had a blade or something seriously sharp on it to cause this damage. I hear a wet thunk and look down the road. A PC has ended the Z, stomping its head to mush.

"Guess I can't ask it why it wanted to play in traffic," I say.

"Yes, because that's a good use of our time," Stuart says as he comes up to me bouncing the spare. "So is changing a tire in an unsecured area."

No sooner does he say that than a small horde of Zs come lurching down from a parking lot of what used to be a Texas Roadhouse restaurant. There's close to twenty of them and the PCs get ready. Some sling their rifles and snap out their sharpened, collapsible batons.

Ah, the collapsible baton. It's the go to weapon of choice nowadays. We've pretty much given up on the boards with nails and sharpened rebar. The PCs have brought a sense of professionalism to the zombie apocalypse. Which is nice.

Quickly and fairly quietly, the PCs close on the horde. They have a system that's pretty ingenious. The first PC cracks his or her baton against the knees of the first Z, crippling it and sending it tumbling to the pavement. The second PC comes along and stabs the Z in the head, killing it instantly. Or killing it again, I guess. They do this in waves: first PC hits knees, second kills Z, third hits knees, fourth kills Z, and so on.

It's an assembly line of Z death. Pretty simple, really.

Unless you add the chaos of reality to things.

Which, of course, happens.

The first PC cripples a Z and the second PC kills it. First PC cripples a Z, but it won't go down. WTF? He whacks it again and the thing still won't go down. It runs into the PC, rotten hands clawing at the man's body armor. So the PC flips the thing over and slams it to the ground. That's when the Z's prosthetic leg snaps off at the thigh and rolls down the hill towards the truck.

This seemingly innocuous change in routine turns into a nightmare. The first PC has his back turned to the horde, which is a no-no, because he had to change tactics and flip the peg-legged Z. He doesn't see how close the others are. Sure, the guy knows they're coming, but because they are on a downhill slope, he misjudges the speed at which they are coming. He's tackled about the waist and goes down hard.

The second PC starts in with the skull crushing as the first PC starts in with the screaming. Batons go away fast and back come the rifles. The gunfire makes me jump as I get the truck jacked up and start in on the lug nuts. Stuart just stands close to me, his 9mm Beretta raised and ready.

"Anytime now, Jace," he says. I hear the judgmental coolness in his tone.

"You ever try taking off lug nuts with one fucking hand?" I snap. "No. No, you haven't. You know that horse you rode in on? You're welcome to saddle back up and fuck it."

He just glares.

"Great, I'm on your shit list now?" I ask as I crank the lug wrench. "All I did was lose control for three seconds and give that bitch a piece of my mind."

"Which is why Stella is in charge and you're not," he replies.

The lug nuts drop to the ground and start rolling away, but Stuart corrals them with his feet, making sure I see the look of disdain on his face. Why do haters gotta hate? Don't answer that.

I yank the flat off the rim and toss it up into the truck bed. I get the spare on, with a little help, tighten the lug nuts and then let the jack down. All in all it took me eight minutes. And in those eight minutes one man was killed and the rest are busy fighting off an ever growing horde of Zs.

"Holy shit," Julio says as he jumps down from the truck bed. "Where the hell did they all come from?"

The truck cab opens and Elsbeth steps out, her blades in hand. The woman loves her some blades.

"I have the engine going," Melissa says. "Get clear and get back in here. We don't have time for this fight."

"Won't take long," Elsbeth says as she jogs then sprints towards the fray.

The PCs are spinning about, back to back, shoulder to shoulder, their rifles obliterating Z heads. But there are so many. Elsbeth slides into the horde and begins to sever heads from necks. I watch, fascinated, as Z heads, their teeth still gnashing, come rolling down the hill like giant, bloody acorns dropped from a devil oak.

"Hurry up, buttercup," Stuart says as he starts shooting the heads. "Gotta do your part."

There are Z heads all around me. I step over one then kind of bend and lean down, piercing its brain with Stumpageddon's Mr.

Spikey. I do this over and over and over until my side is about to cramp up and my shoulder feels like molten lead. The pain in my stump is excruciating and it gets harder and harder to finish off a new head.

Then it all stops and I'm left ankle deep in rotten, bloated, severed Z heads. Stuart pats me on the back and walks back to the truck. He jumps into the bed, gives Julio a hand up, and then slumps down. The PCs follow, with their fallen comrade in their arms. Everyone is secured and I realize they're all staring at me.

"Right," I whisper, "sorry."

Elsbeth gives me a weak smile as she gets into the backseat of the cab and I hop back in front.

"Where'd they all come from?" Mindy asks as Melissa gets us moving again.

"The hotel back behind the steakhouse," Melissa says. "Hard to see with the trees all grown up around it. They must have been trapped inside and finally broke free. We just happened to be here when they did."

"Sorry," I mutter.

"Well, you should be," Brenda snaps. "If you had more self-control you'd know that insulting and attacking me was..."

The sentence ends abruptly with a cry of pain as Elsbeth punches her across the face. She grabs Brenda's shirt and yanks her close, their noses almost touching.

"Shut. Up," Elsbeth snarls, "or you walk."

Brenda almost can't help herself and I can see her mouth start to open in response, but the look in Elsbeth's eyes is not a look you argue with. Brenda's mouth closes quickly and she swats at Elsbeth's iron grip.

"Let her go, El," I say. "It's over."

Elsbeth lets the evil bitch go and leans back into the seat. I just turn and look out the windshield.

We head down Hendersonville Rd at a steady pace, all eyes on the sides looking for more stragglers that could impede our progress. While we were busy fighting the horde, Shumway was busy texting his intense displeasure at us not being there yet. It sounds like the situation has deteriorated quickly.

I'm sure each of us has some image of how bad the situation is at the power plant, since we've all been living this nightmare for years and we aren't new to the horrors of the zombie apocalypse. But as we turn onto Long Shoals Rd and get about a quarter mile along we see just how wrong all of our expectations are.

"Oh, my God," Brenda says, her voice small and childlike, not like her usual bitch bluster.

"I'll second that," I say. It's probably the first (and last) time I'll ever agree with Brenda Kelly again.

The road is swarmed. It's shoulder to shoulder covered with Zs. They are packed so tight I don't know where one ends and another begins.

Melissa slams on the brakes, which normally would have elicited protests from anyone riding in the truck bed. This time there's only stunned silence as we all look at the wall of undead before us.

Then it turns, that wall of undead, almost as one. And looks right at us.

"Move," I whisper.

Melissa keeps staring ahead, her hands gripping the steering wheel until her knuckles pop.

"Mel," I say, my voice a little stronger, "get us out of here."

"What about the plant?" she asks as she's already shifting into reverse.

"The plant's lost," I say, "just go."

"We're going to leave them?" Mindy asks.

My guess is she's thinking out loud. There's no way, not with the number of Zs we are staring at, that anyone can possibly think we have a chance of getting through to the power plant. And even if we did, then what? We get trapped along with Shumway and his crew?

It's over.

"It's over," I say. "Back to Whispering Pines. Back home. Now."

I look behind us and see Stuart, Julio, and the PCs all crouched down in the truck bed, ready for what comes next. Which is Melissa speeding backwards and then hitting the brakes and cranking on the wheel. The truck spins about and we are pointing towards Hendersonville Rd once more.

None of us say a thing as we speed away from the power plant. There's nothing we can say or nothing we want to say. Better to internalize what just happened and lock it away deep down for a while.

Better to just get home and then figure it all out.

CHAPTER THREE

"Holy fuck," Melissa grunts as she stops the truck.

"I don't think your daddy would approve of that language," I say. She gives me a look and I shut up.

"That must be the horde from the steakhouse," Mindy says. "Right?"

"No," I say, pointing, "see the overpass? They're dropping down from I-40. Look at them all."

We do.

A banging on top of the cab pulls us all out of our shock. The back window slides open.

"As fascinating as this is," Stuart snaps, "we need to haul ass out of here."

"Where?" Melissa asks, looking over her shoulder at him. "We can't go back."

"We go left," Julio says.

"That's just medical offices and shit," I say, "there's no road there.

"Don't need a road," Julio says, "just need to get moving."

"What's on the other side?" Melissa asks.

"The Biltmore," I say. I give Stuart and Julio a hard look. "You want us to go onto the Biltmore grounds? It's covered with Zs!"

"True," Stuart nods, "but we think there's a trick to that."

"There is," Elsbeth says, "they're right. We should go there. Maybe the girls will help us."

"The girls?" I ask. "The ones you've been following? How do we know they're not going to kill us and eat us?"

Elsbeth glares. "Why? Because I was a canny, you think they are? You're a bigot."

"I'm not a bigot," I snap. "I'm just being cautious. We don't know shit about..."

"We have no time for this!" Stuart shouts. "They're getting closer! Mel, punch it and get us up that hill and towards the Biltmore!"

Melissa turns the wheel and aims for the drive that leads up to a huge parking lot for the medical office complex at the top of the hill. We drive parallel with I-40 and as we climb the hill, we can see more and more of what we are up against.

Hundreds of Zs.

No, no, let me back up because that's just my fear trying to keep it together. We don't see hundreds.

We see thousands.

A small squeak from behind me tells me Mindy Starling can count too. Good for her.

"That's a lot of death," Elsbeth says.

"No shit, girl," Melissa says. "Oh, fuck!"

Melissa slams on the brakes and my forehead slams into the dashboard. A little painful example of cause and effect. Even in the apocalypse, one should wear their seatbelt. Ouch.

"Madre de Dios," Julio says from the window. "Can you get us around? Over there. See!"

The parking lot is swarmed with Zs. They're scaling the other side of the hill that butts up against I-40. We can't go forward except for a drainage ditch that Julio is pointing at.

"Do it," I say to Melissa. "Follow the ditch. Get us out of here."

The truck lurches forward and Melissa turns it towards the ditch. The swarm of Zs is almost on us and the PCs start to open fire, hoping to give us a little breathing room and a head start. The front wheels ram up and over the curb that borders the ditch and Melissa cranks the wheel to the left, hoping to give us the angle we need to avoid-.

"Fuck!" Melissa shouts. "We're stuck!"

The truck bottoms out on the curb as the front end goes over, the undercarriage catching on the cement. She pushes her foot to the floor, hoping to get some traction, but the truck is rear wheel drive and those rear wheels are about a quarter inch off the ground.

"Everyone up against the tailgate!" Melissa shouts.

"Good idea," I say, "that'll redistribute the weight so the tires can touch again."

Then it hits me. The physics of what's about to happen.

"No! Wait!" I yell just as the rear tires touch asphalt.

The truck shoots forward and everyone that wasn't hanging on tight in the bed goes tumbling over the tailgate. I hear the thuds of bodies against pavement, but can't focus on that. I have to focus on the line of trees that's rocketing towards us. Or, I guess, we're the ones rocketing towards the trees.

"SHIIIIIIIIIIIIIIIT!" I scream and am joined by similar sentiments as the truck smashes into a couple of small pines.

The trees snap in half and we keep going, but not very far, as we wedge between two larger pines. The truck comes to a jarring halt and steam geysers out from under the hood.

"Everyone out!" I yell. "Go, go, go!"

Elsbeth is already out of the truck and sprinting back up the hill.

"El! Stop!" I shout as I race after her.

"Jace! Where the hell are you going?" Melissa yells as she helps Brenda and Mindy out of the truck. Blood is pouring down her face from a nasty gash across her forehead, but she ignores the wound, her eyes locked onto me. "Get your ass back here, Long Pork!"

PCs that didn't fall out start moving the women the rest of the way down the hill towards a large iron fence at the bottom. The border of the Biltmore estate.

I keep climbing, scrambling back up the hill to the parking lot. A wail of agony blasts across the landscape and I fear I know why. I know that voice.

"No! NO NO NO!" Elsbeth screams as I crest the hill and see her kneeling next to Julio's broken body.

His head is at an unnatural angle and blood pools everywhere. She reaches for him, about to touch his face, but pulls her hand back. Stuart, busy helping two PCs carry another PC with a snapped leg, looks at me, down at Julio, and then over his shoulder at the parking lot swarm that has skipped horde status and gone right to a full on herd.

"We have thirty seconds," Stuart says, his face a rictus of pain and grief. "Don't let her fall behind."

"Jesus," I say as I crouch next to Elsbeth. "I'm sorry, El. I'm so sorry."

She pulls one of her blades and places the tip to Julio's temple. I can see her strain with the effort to administer the final, killing blow. The stab that will make sure Julio doesn't come back a Z.

"I...can't...," she says, turning to me. Her eyes. Oh, God, her eyes. I've never seen more pain in my life.

And that's saying a lot.

"I got it," I say, "go with the others."

"No," she says as she shoves the blade in my hand and stands up, her other blade drawn. "They pay."

I don't need the blade, since Stumpageddon is in Mr. Spikey drag and all, and I try to hand it back, but she's gone.

"El! No!" I yell as she runs towards the herd of Zs. "God DAMMIT! COME BACK!"

But she doesn't come back. She dives into the herd and all I see is black blood and chaos. Limbs start flying everywhere, heads shooting up into the air, the moans of the Zs turn into a herd-wide guttural roar.

There's nothing I can do.

I take El's blade and make good on her final request. I plunge the steel deep into Julio's brain. Blood gushes out around the metal and onto my hand.

"Goodbye, man," I say, "you will be missed."

Wiping the blade on my jeans, I slide it into my belt, stand up, turn, and look at the herd coming towards me. I can see the swath of destruction Elsbeth is wreaking on the Zs, but I can't see Elsbeth. She's lost in the death. I almost wonder if she hasn't always been.

"El!" I shout, but regret it as the front wave of Zs turn their attention away from the mad canny and on me. "Oh...poop."

This isn't the point where I dive in after her. This isn't the point where I say, "Fuck it" and sacrifice myself in one big, last blaze of glory. No, I'm not that guy.

I turn and sprint towards the drainage ditch, leaping over the curb and coming down hard on the side of the hill. My feet almost go out from under me, but I manage a controlled slide down to the truck.

Everyone's gone. The truck is empty. No people and no gear.

"Shit," I say as I push forward towards the estate.

I shove past small pines and thorny underbrush. Which brings me to one of my pet peeves about North Carolina: why the fuck does every fucking bush have to have giant, fucking thorns? What's with this state? We have pitcher plants and Venus flytraps that are fucking carnivorous. And every last bush has thorns on it. It's like we're one nuclear radiation accident away from a plant uprising. It's totally messed up.

Said despised thorns tear at my clothes and my skin, leaving me slashed and cut to shit by the time I break free of the grove of pines and find everyone else.

And, oh look, they have found some folks too.

"Where's our sister?" A tall, lanky brunette with a nasty scar across her forehead asks me as she shoves past my people. "Did you leave her?"

"I...uh...she...well," I stammer, "who are you?"

"Doesn't matter," the young woman says, "where is she?"

I nod back over my shoulder. "She wouldn't come with me," I say. "She just went nuts and decided to take on the whole herd."

"Fucking A," Stuart says.

"You didn't even try to stop her?" Brenda asks. Guess she has her bitchiness back.

"Are you fucking kidding me?" I snap. "I couldn't stop her anymore than I can stop that fucking herd!"

"Stacy, Lacy, Tracy," the brunette orders, "with me. Antoinette, Belinda, stay here and watch the people. If we don't come back...kill them. They left our sister."

"Whoa, whoa, whoa," I say as the brunette, and who I assume are Stacy, Tracy, and Lacy, run into the pine grove and up the hill. "Hold on!"

I don't know why, but I follow. Back into the fucking thorns. Fucking. Thorns.

"Wait!" I yell. They don't.

They're past the truck and running straight up the hill. No slipping, no stumbling, no hesitation. Their legs and arms pump and before I'm at the truck they are out of sight, up over the curb.

I have to go hand over spike to keep myself from slipping back down, but I finally make it. And pretty much shit my pants.

There's nothing but Zs before me. And they are fucking close. Like *close* close. Reach out and touch someone close. But that's not what has me wanting to make with the pants shitting. Nope. It's the sight of five young women, *five*, taking on a thousand Zs.

And winning.

Okay, okay, maybe not so much winning as they aren't losing. Which counts as a win in my book. Not that I'm a give everyone a ribbon for participation kind of guy. I'm not. But I'll call not getting eaten right away after jumping into a herd a win. That's fair.

Zs turn, their noses smelling my man-stink, and I gulp. Time to get to work. No days off in the zombie apocalypse, folks. Gotta keep on with the stabby stabby and the slicey slicey and the...god, I'm tired. So fucking tired of this bullshit. It's more than a man can take. I used to handle it. I used to be the big joker. Laugh it off and-
.

"LONG PORK!" Elsbeth screams. "HEAD OUT OF ASS!"

Oh, right. I really pick the shittiest times to space off.

Three Zs reach for me and I yank El's blade from my belt, slicing their hands off at the forearms. I slam the spike into the eye socket of one then another, but don't have time to get the third before it's on me. It moves quickly, but trips over the curb, slamming into my chest and sending us both tumbling down the hill. We go end over end. Feet up, heads up, feet up, heads up, feet up, heads- OW! FUCK!

My head slams into the rear bumper of the truck and stars explode in my vision. Vision that's taken up by the wide open, very hungry mouth of a Z.

"Fuck you," I snarl as I put the spike to the son of a bitch's temple.

But the fucker shifts and the spike just glances off its skull, tearing matted hair and gray skin. It snaps at me, its jaws clamping onto my shoulder. I scream at the pain and shove as hard as I can, pushing the Z off me. Damn, those fuckers' jaws are strong! I have never understood how they can be dead, but bite with the strength of a rabid pitbull. Fuckers.

It rolls to the side then scrambles at me. The thing is pretty fast, so it must be recently deceased. I'm guessing by the farm attire that it's a local that got caught up in the herd. That's the dangerous thing about herds: they are self-perpetuating. They come down so hard on an area that they are able to add to the numbers quickly. And numbers that were overwhelming at first become mindboggling within days.

My mind is pretty fucking boggled.

The spike pierces the forehead of the Z and it stops dead (ha ha ha) a foot from me. I yank Stumpageddon back, which isn't so easy with the connected shoulder feeling like I just got kicked by a horse, and the thing falls flat on its rotted face. Reaching back, I find the truck's bumper and pull myself to my feet. My head and shoulder hurt like a motherfuck, but I shake the pain off (ow) and start back up the hill (ow). No way I'm leaving Elsbeth on her own.

There's even more. More Zs. More death. More blood. More everything. More rage? Yeah, more of that, too.

The women work as a unit, even Elsbeth. They cut and stab and crack and snap and break and kill and kill and kill; swirling about each other in a complex ballet of flashing metal and raging war cries. Without having to think or coordinate, each woman knows when to duck, when to kick, when to pull back. They are a synchronized killing machine.

"Get down, dipshit," Stuart hisses from behind me.

I've been around the man long enough not to argue. My body flattens against the pavement as he and the PCs open fire, taking out the periphery of the herd as it starts to close around the women. They don't even look our way, just keep killing. Boots pass by my head and I glance up to see the rest of the women hurrying into the battle. Stuart and the PCs make sure their fire is aimed only to the sides, and the occasional stupid Z that wants to come right at us.

In seconds, there's a nice ring of Z bodies piled up on the pavement, slowing down the rest of the herd and keeping it from over taking us all.

"Get your ass back here," Stuart snaps as he grabs my ankle. I scoot back over the curb and smile. He doesn't smile back. "You are such a pain in my ass, Stanford."

Oh, the last name treatment. He's mad.

"Sorry," I mumble.

"Get down there and make sure Brenda doesn't do anything stupid. It's only her, Mindy, and Melissa with Lenny."

"Who?"

"The wounded PC!" Stuart snarls.

"Oh."

I can never remember their names.

"Get going!" Stuart orders. "Who knows what idiocy is going through that woman's brain."

"What could she do?" I ask.

"Do you really want to find out?" Stuart says as he resumes firing. "Go!"

Once last glance at Elsbeth and the Super Chick Fighting Force, and I'm sliding (again!) down the hill, past the truck, and into the pines. Thorns, thorns, thorns, and free.

Dammit, I hate it when Stuart is right about bad things.

"What the fuck are you doing?" I yell at Brenda as I watch her holding a pistol on Melissa. "Have you lost your mind?"

"Look in there!" Brenda screeches, pointing at the fields beyond the iron fence. "She wants us to go in there! Look at the Zs! They're everywhere!"

"You stupid cow," Melissa snarls, her eyes locked onto the pistol. "You heard what Stuart said. The Zs don't move! Look at them! They're staked or something to the ground!"

I look past Brenda's bulk and see the hundreds of Zs spread out across the overgrown field. Melissa's right, they are swaying and reaching and moaning, but aren't moving from their spots. It is like they're glued in place.

"I think we should listen," Mindy says quietly. "Stuart is a smart man, Brenda. He knows Zs."

"And I don't?" she yells. "I've been in this apocalypse just as long as he has! I've fought Zs! I know how to survive! And you don't survive by going into a field that's filled with Zs! That's suicide!"

The gunfire behind us stops and I start to look back that way. So does Brenda. That gives Melissa her chance and she takes it. Lunging forward, Melissa smacks Brenda's hand, pushing the pistol down.

Bang!

"Oh!" Brenda yells as the gun barks in her hand.

Melissa grabs her wrist and tries to take the pistol, but Brenda actually has some fight in her. I never knew. Not that I'm impressed. I'm not. The woman could fart the Star Spangled Banner out her tight ass and I'd still think she was a worthless blob of shit. But I didn't know she could fight.

Brenda's heel slams down on Melissa's foot, then her elbow slams back into Mel's gut. It gives her the space she needs as Melissa stumbles back just a fraction of an inch. Brenda raises the gun and fires. But Mel is faster. Years of being in charge of the scavengers and having to go outside Whispering Pines on life and death runs has made the woman's reflexes top notch. The bullet whizzes past Melissa's shoulder as she dodges to the side. Without wasting a millisecond, she lets loose with a haymaker that makes my teeth rattle just from watching it connect with Brenda's jaw.

The fat cow spins about, staggers a foot or two, and then goes down on her hands and knees. Melissa kicks her in the ass, sending her forward onto her face. I rush forward and snag the pistol, tucking it into my waistband as I step away from the beached whale.

Don't get me wrong, I'm not making fun of her because of her weight; I'm just trying to make it known how little humanity the wildebeest has in her.

Which is insulting to wildebeests and whales I guess. My apologies to all wildebeests and whales. If they still exist.

"I should kill her right now," Melissa says as Brenda rolls onto her back, her eyes wide with a mix of fear and absolute hatred.

"Jace?" Mindy says behind us. "Melissa?"

We both turn and our eyes go as wide as Brenda's.

56

"Oh, shit," I whisper as Melissa quickly covers the ground between Mindy and us. "Oh, shit."

Mindy is on her knees, her hands clutching her belly, dark red blood spilling over her knuckles.

"It hurts," Mindy says, "a lot."

"Just hold on," Melissa says as she kneels in front of Mindy, her eyes studying the wound. "Keep your hands pressed against your belly."

"I can't," Mindy says, wincing. "It really hurts. And this happens." She bravely presses down and blood gushes out from between her hands like a river breaking through a kid's mud damn. She looks at Melissa then her eyes find mine. "Am I going to die?"

"No, no, we'll help you," I reply. "We'll stop the bleeding and get you all patched up. I was shot in the gut remember, and I'm all good."

"Jace," Melissa whispers.

"No, no, don't worry," I continue. "We can get you to Whispering Pines. Dr. McCormick will stitch up that little ol' flesh wound. No problem."

"Jace, stop," Melissa says, sighing as she gets to her feet.

"What? Why?" I ask. Then I see.

When your friends or family can come back from the dead to eat your ass, you learn the signs of a person passing. Mindy has passed. Her butt rests back on her calves, and because of her bulk, she stays in that position even though the life has left her. Her eyes are glazed and her chest isn't moving. Then, like watching an avalanche in slow motion, she slumps to the side and hits the ground with a sad, quiet thunk.

"You fucking bitch!" I yell as I spin about and lock eyes with Brenda. "She didn't deserve that! See what happens! SEE!" I stomp towards the woman and she gives a frightened squeak as she tries to scurry away on her hands and ass, but only gets so far as she comes up against the wounded PC's body. "That should be you there! YOU!"

"I didn't...I...it was your fault!" she cries out.

This stops me in my tracks. What the what?

"My fault?" I say. "Are you fucking serious?"

She keeps scuttling back and her face scrunches up in that self-righteous way it does when she's ready to spit and fight even though she knows (does she?) that she's wrong.

"You started all of this! You and Stuart and that cannibal cunt! None of this would have happened if you'd just listened to me back when... AAAAAAAAAAAHHHHHH!"

I jump back when she screams, but Melissa hurries forward, grabs the pistol from my waistband, and puts a bullet in the brain of the PC that has its jaws clamped around Brenda's neck. The new Z/former ally falls backwards and Brenda slaps her hand against the wound. Only a little blood trickles from between her fingers, so the thing didn't get an artery, but it still gave her a nice death hickey.

"Oh, no," Brenda whispers. "No, no, no, no, no..."

"Shut up!" Melissa shouts as she slaps Brenda across the face. "You reap what you sow, bitch!"

"What the fuck is going on?" Stuart yells as he bursts from the pines with the young women and only one PC. "Stop bickering and get your asses over that fence!"

The women, Elsbeth with them, hurry to the fence and half squat down, their hands interlaced. The rest place boots in the hands and are helped up over the fence.

"Come on!" the one I think is called Lacy shouts.

One by one, they hop over until all that's left is the brunette and Elsbeth.

"Your turn, Long Pork," Elsbeth says, squatting down.

I don't argue and take the help and clamber up over the iron fence. I don't look anywhere as cool as the women did. But I get over. Elsbeth helps Melissa and then the brunette.

"Let's go, Ms. Kelly," Stuart says. "Get off your ass."

"Leave her," Melissa says, "she's been bitten."

Stuart takes a step back, but Elsbeth steps forward. The smile on Elsbeth's face would make the Joker shiver.

"You're dead," Elsbeth says, leaning in close so that her forehead is touching Brenda's. "Bye bye."

"Move," Stuart says, pulling his Beretta, "I'll make it quick."

"No," Elsbeth says, grabbing the gun from Stuart's grip and tossing it over the fence. One of the girls (Stacy?) catches it easily.

"What the hell, Elsbeth?" Stuart snaps.

Snarls and groans come from the pines and the first wave of Zs stumble from the grove. They're moving quickly from their momentum downhill and Stuart and Elsbeth only have seconds.

"Let's go!" I shout. "Stuart! El! Come on!"

Stuart makes a move towards Brenda, but Elsbeth blocks his way. She points at the fence. They face off for an eternity, but Stuart finally relents and grabs onto the fence. He's able to get himself over and lands close to me.

"Wait," Brenda pleads, her eyes going from us, to Elsbeth, to the Zs, and back to us. "You...you can't leave me!"

"We can," Elsbeth says as she climbs up and over. "We did."

"No! No, you can't!" Brenda screams, getting to her feet. Her hand falls away from her neck and blood spurts out in short, quick bursts. I guess the PC did hit an artery after all. She doesn't even notice the heartbeat driven spurts as she grabs the thick, iron bars of the fence. "Please! Don't leave me to those things! PLEASE!"

We all watch; what else can we do? The Zs close on her in seconds and she wails with terror and pain. Hands grab her as jaws go to rip her apart.

The gunshot makes all of us jump.

"She learned fear," Elsbeth says as she hands me the smoking pistol. "Here."

Brenda's body falls dead under the wave of Zs that slam into the fence. Most swarm over her corpse, hungry for a taste, but some of the greedier ones try to reach through the fence at us. They want the fresh stuff. Looks like even the undead have food snobs. Eat fresh, eat local, eat the living and all that.

"Anyone else bitten?" the brunette asks.

Everyone shakes their head. I do too, but maybe a split second too late. Elsbeth narrows her eyes at me. I smile and give her my best "What?" look.

"Fine," the brunette nods, "come with us. You're safe."

I've been living in the zombie apocalypse for years and never have those words been true. I doubt they are now. Especially as we start to walk towards the field of Zs in front of us.

"Uh, I don't think your definition of safe is the same as mine," I say.

"Just stay close," the woman says, "step where we step. Keep your arms in tight. Be alert. You'll be fine."

At first, it's like an undead, claustrophobic nightmare. We're shoulder to shoulder at times with Zs, but it only takes a couple twists and turns before I see the genius behind the design. The placement of the Zs is brilliantly random yet perfectly organized. There is a path if you know what you are looking for. Kind of like hiking on an old, overgrown mountain trail, except the trail would really like to eat you, please.

The arms of the Zs that line the "trail" are stitched to their sides. Even if they wanted to, and they sooooo want to, they can't grab you. Their mouths aren't stitched though, so I have to stop gawking and duck more than once.

"How long did it take you to do this?" I ask.

"As long as it needed to take," a woman in front of me says. She's blonde, blue eyed, and tone like I've never seen. She has muscles that make Elsbeth look like a soccer mom gone to seed. "We didn't count."

"Oh, yeah, sorry," I say.

She glances over her shoulder and gives me a quick smile. "Don't be," she says. "It's just that time is an irrelevant concept these days. Why bother with how long a task takes when all that matters is you get it done? Who are we competing against?" She nods at the Zs that hiss and moan around us. "Them? They don't know what time even is so why should we? It's an outdated concept."

"Uh…yeah. Cool," I nod, "you've thought about this a lot."

"What's a lot?" the woman asks. "Why give in to a need to quantify quantity when…"

"Antoinette?" the brunette asks.

"Yes, Cassie?" the young woman, Antoinette, replies.

"Stop fucking with the survy," she says, "you'll break his brain. Then we'll have to deal with a jelly head."

"My bady bad," Antoinette shrugs. "Hope I didn't break your brain."

"Not likely," I say. "I have a reputation as being kind of a genius." Stuart snorts. "What?"

"You have a reputation for being a dumbass," he says. "You're great at solving problems, but so are mice in a maze looking for cheese."

Ouch.

"Well, I don't think a canny girl is going to break my brain, at least," I say.

The whole group stops and I walk right into the back of Antoinette. It's like walking into a brick wall with a layer of cotton over it.

"Shit," I say. "I put my foot in my mouth, didn't I?"

"We aren't cannies," the brunette, Cassie, says, "never have been, never will be."

"Oh, sorry," I say. "I just assumed since...well... you know."

"No, I don't know," Cassie says, her hands on her hips. A Z leans over for a taste of her shoulder and she swats him away like he's nothing to be bothered by. "Please explain, Mr. Long Pork."

I look at Stuart for help but he just shakes his head. "Dumbass."

"I mean, uh, well you're out here alone and I'm sure you've run through your supplies," I start. "And you're all pretty badass, kinda like...well...uh..."

"Like me?" Elsbeth asks. "Is that what you mean, *Mr*. Long Pork?"

Yep. Dumbass.

"I'm sorry," I say, raising my hands up in a placating gesture. My shoulder stings and I wince. "I made an assumption and was wrong. Won't happen again."

"Yeah, right," Melissa scoffs.

I have absolutely zero allies right now. It's lonely being Mr. Long Pork.

"Apology accepted," Cassie nods. And then she's off again.

Elsbeth watches me for second before turning around. I'm pretty sure she glanced at my shoulder when I winced. Not like there's a problem. I'm sure it's just bruised when that Z bit me. As long as there aren't any holes in my shirt I'm all good, right?

Right?

We keep moving and the sun beats down on us. It's late afternoon (I'm still hanging onto my concept of time) and the sun is right in my face. I shield my eyes, making sure to keep my elbow tucked in and away from any hungry mouths, and stumble along.

Then it's there, up on the horizon overlooking us all.

The Biltmore House.

"Home sweet home," one of the women says. "I'll let them know we have friendlies. The others will be happy to have guests."

She takes off up the slight incline, sprinting towards the side of what had been called America's Largest Home. The rest of us take it slow and hike our way around overgrown statutes and long dead topiaries.

"When we get inside you'll wait by the atrium," Cassie says. "Don't wander. Don't go exploring. Stay put. Understood?"

We all agree, even Stuart. He saw what they can do and I doubt he wants to go from being one of the friendlies to one of the foes.

Neither do I.

***

The Biltmore was started in 1889 and finished in 1895. It's over 178,000 square feet and until Z-Day was the largest privately owned residence in America. Like the Grove Park Inn, it was a favorite place for Stella and me to bring the kids. We'd come every year to see the Christmas trees and throughout the year just to hang out in the gardens and the grounds. We had passes. It was cool.

So I'm quite familiar with the atrium that is off to the right as you first come in. But not in its present state. It explains why they don't need to be cannies. The place is chock full of fruit vines and rows of vegetables. Certainly doesn't hurt that the atrium in the Biltmore House is almost as big as my entire house back at Whispering Pines. Man, if they have this here I wonder what they have growing down in the massive greenhouses by the gardens.

"You know, I haven't ever been in here," Stuart says.

"What? Not even pre-Z?" Melissa asks. "Shoot, Stuart, I've been to this house a hundred times. Jon and I used to come here. He loved the architecture."

"Yeah, he did," I say. It's hard hearing about Jon. The man was my best friend in Whispering Pines. Being killed by Vance was not the way to go. I miss that bastard. Jon, not Vance. I don't miss Vance. I could totally do without Vance.

"Where's Elsbeth?" Stuart asks. "She was right here."

"I have a feeling she has some business with our hosts," I say. "I have zero clue what exactly that business is, but she's connected to them somehow. Just like she was connected to Ms. Foster."

"You know Ms. Foster?" a voice asks behind us. We all jump. Damn, these women are quiet.

"Uh, well, I didn't like *know* her know her," I say as I turn around, "but we met and hung out for a bit."

This young woman is a skinny redhead with freckles covering almost every inch of her that isn't covered by her tank top and jean shorts. She smiles at us then steps forward and offers her hand.

"I'm Brittany," she says as she shakes each of our hands.

"Brittany?" Melissa laughs. "Stacy, Tracy, Lacy, Antoinette, Cassie. It's like we stepped into a post-apocalyptic sorority."

"We're sisters, if that's what you mean," Brittany says. "Not blood sisters. Stronger than that. Ms. Foster brought us together and-."

"That's enough, Brit," Cassie says as she comes walking down the grand staircase with Elsbeth at her side and nine other young women behind her.

I recognize Antoinette and the Lacy/Stacy/Tracy trio, but some of the others are new. All are dressed in summer casual- shorts, t-shirts, tank tops, sandals, hiking shoes. But every one of them look like they can crush me if I step out of line.

"Let's get our guests settled and fed before we go into details," Cassie says. "There's food this way."

She walks past the atrium to two wide doors that lead into what I think is a long sitting room. There are a few tables set up with fruits and veggies and even bread and what looks like jam. Fresh jam! Plus jugs of water. Everyone quickly moves towards the refreshments, but my attention is on the large wood doors closed at the very end of the room. I know that's the library.

"Are there still books in there?" I ask, nodding towards the library. "I've always wanted to be able to go through them."

"Why wouldn't there be books?" Cassie asks. "No reason to get rid of them."

"I just didn't know if you'd used them as firewood or something," I say.

"Or something?" Cassie smiles. "Like what? Building forts? Propping up wobbly tables?"

"No need to bust his balls," Stuart says, "the guy likes books. That's all."

Cassie smiles at Stuart, but there's no warmth behind it. Stuart returns the smile in kind.

"Go ahead," Cassie says, nodding towards the door. "Knock yourself out, genius."

"Um, okay," I say as I scoop up a handful of grapes and some apple slices and walk towards the big doors. I look over my shoulder, but no one is coming with; they're all just watching me. "Gonna just pop in and check out the library now. Let me know when it's time for tea."

"We're having tea," Brittany says. "Doesn't he know that?"

I'm very confused by everything.

The doors open easily and then I'm standing in the Biltmore library. No ropes, no attendants, no video cameras to keep me back. Just the books and me.

I cram the grapes in my mouth and wipe my hand on my pants. Then I realize just how dirty my hand is. God, I can't touch these books. Not with a hand like this. I mean one shelf must be worth a million dollars alone.

Which makes me laugh because nothing is worth a million dollars anymore. Not post-Z. I can touch whatever I want without having to worry about the consequences. Uh, that doesn't sound right. You know what I mean. Shut up.

Volumes of Chaucer and Shakespeare. Histories of ancient Greece, Europe, America. Tomes containing outdated science and philosophy. Over 10,000 books all at my grubby fingertips.

I'm in heaven. I could spend the rest of my life sitting in this one room. Just get me a chamber pot and bring me my meals and I'll never leave. Oh, and open some windows; it's a tad musty.

Then it hits me: the secret door!

There's a secret door on the second floor that leads directly to George Vanderbilt's room. I am so gonna find that sucker and do some snooping. Glancing about, I hurry over to the spiral staircase across the room. Up I go and begin my search.

"Oh, secret door. Where are you?" I whisper. "Wait, I know." I walk to the side of the grand fireplace and tap at the wall. It takes me a minute, but I find a small indentation and I press. There's a click and a skinny panel cracks open slightly. I give it a push and peek inside.

Stairs. Excellent.

"Eh hem," a voice behind me says, "I said the library, not the rest of the house."

Cassie is directly behind me, looking bored.

"Yeah, I, uh, well," I say. Oh, screw it. "I just wanted to go through the secret door. That's all. I've been on this tour a billion times and this is like Disneyland to me. Can I just check it out?"

Cassie watches me for a second then smiles. It's a real, genuine smile.

"The secret doors are my favorite," Cassie says as she pushes past me. "Come on. I'll show you."

She takes my hand and leads me up the stairs. It's dark and dusty, but it isn't long before she opens another door and leads us right into a passageway that opens into George Vanderbilt's bedroom. The place is a mess, covered in clothes and boots and various piles of gear.

"Sorry," she says. "I keep meaning to pick up, but never do. Kinda wish this place still had servants. Wouldn't that be cool?"

"Let me move in and I'll give you my kids," I say.

"You have kids?" she asks. "How many?"

"Boy and a girl. Both teenagers," I say.

"Oh, that's right," she nods. "Charlie and Greta. They're back at Whispering Pines with your wife Stella?"

Do I need to say my jaw drops and I stand there staring like a boob?

Cassie laughs and slaps me on my shoulder. I wince. She frowns.

"You okay?" she asks.

"Just surprised you know who my family is," I say.

"We know all about you," she replies. "You've been taking care of our sister for us, so it's just right to know everything there is to know about the Stanfords."

"Yeah, sure, of course," I nod. "Silly me."

Not creepy. Nope. Not creepy at all.

"I've freaked you out, huh?" she says. "Sorry. It's just that we don't have much to do other than explore Asheville and keep tabs on everyone." She leans in. "You ever run into Knockers downtown?"

"Knockers? Uh, no, can't say that I have."

"Oh, she's great," Cassie says. "Lives in the basement of City Hall. Beds down between some old filing cabinets. Talks to herself non-stop. We still can't figure out how she hasn't been eaten. She never shuts up. But when the Zs come she disappears."

"Why do you call her Knockers?" I ask.

"Oh, because she has these huge, saggy tits that drop down to her waist," Cassie laughs. "She must be seventy years old. Took her bra off when Z-Day hit and hasn't put it back on since. We drop food off to her so she stops trying to eat other survies."

"Survies?" I ask.

"Survivors."

"Oh, I get it. Any other nicknames for the Ashevillians out there?"

"Idiots we call meat. Not because we want to eat them, but because that's all they're good for. Whether for the Zs or cannies."

That makes me shiver. She sees it and smiles.

"Don't let it get to you," she says. "But, really, if you get a chance be sure and look for Knockers. She's hilarious."

"Great. Can't wait to meet her," I say. "So…this is your room?"

"Yep."

"Are you like the leader or something?"

"Not really," she shrugs, "we don't have a leader. I'm just kind of in charge because I'm good at it."

"Like my wife," I say. "We're partners in every sense of the word, but when the shit really hits the fan, she's got the last say. Works for me."

"Works for my sisters, too," Cassie responds.

"Yeah, about the sister thing. Uh. What's up with that? You guys aren't really sisters, right?"

"No, not really," Cassie says. "Maybe we should go downstairs so all your friends hear it together."

"Cool."

We go back down the secret passageway (I insist since it's a freakin' secret passageway!) and make our way into the sitting room. Everyone is sitting around, eating fruit and bread and chatting. The women are all seated on the floor, legs crossed, looking back and forth from Stuart to Melissa to the PC (no clue what the guy's name is) and back. They seem to be truly in awe that they have guests.

But most of them keep looking at Elsbeth, who is busy trying to pretend she isn't the object of their attention. Which is weird for Elsbeth. Normally, she'd be all up in someone's face if they kept staring at her. But here? Not so much.

I'm guessing because she lacks the intimidation factor that she has with everyone back at Whispering Pines or the Grove Park. Or she's just freaked out. I know, despite my fun detour to the library, I'm shitting bricks.

"I should introduce us, shouldn't I?" Cassie says. "First, I'm Cassandra, but go by Cassie."

"Hey, Cassie!" the women say and then laugh.

Uh…okay.

She then introduces each of them. Lacy, Tracy, Stacy, Brittany, and Antoinette. Also Dehlia, Marcie, Steph, Belinda, and Audrey. I think Melissa nailed it with the whole sorority names thing.

"And you know Carly here," Cassie smiles, pointing at Elsbeth. "It's great to have her back with the sisters."

"Carly?" I ask. "You mean Elsbeth?"

"That's what she calls herself *now*," Cassie says.

"What Pa called me," Elsbeth says quietly. It's the first she's mentioned Pa in a long time.

The girls all grow tense and quiet. Then they seem to snap out of it and start talking and laughing. I guess introductions are out of the way.

"Okay, now that we're all on a first name basis, how about letting us in on whom you actually are and how you ended up here?" I say.

"Fair enough," Cassie says and starts in on her story. *Their* story.

She talks about being held in a cave or prison or something. About a crazy madman that tortured them, warped them, made them do things, learn things, and...kill things. I can see by the looks on my peeps' faces that I'm not the only one thinking we've walked into some crazy Twilight Zone spy novel thingy.

Then Z-Day. And Ms. Foster.

It all clicks.

What Ms. Foster told me about Elsbeth and why she wanted me to help find her. If Foster'd been straight with me, and told me the real story, things might have gone better. For her and for everyone else. Instead, it led to Ms. Foster losing her head.

Literally.

"We fought our asses off," Cassie says. "Moved from house to house, building to building, always staying barely one step ahead of the Zs. It was months before we made it here." She holds her hands out wide. "They'd already sealed off the grounds, so that was in our favor. But there were all the Zs wandering about."

"It was a long time before we had all of them organized and in place," Brittany laughs. The others laugh with her.

"Pretty good camouflage," Stuart says. "I've been down here dozens of times and never thought it was worth checking out."

"And good job staying off the radar," Melissa ads. "Didn't have a clue someone was living here. Even my uncle, Critter, didn't know."

The women all stop and look at Melissa.

"Critter," Antoinette says. "Wow."

"Wow? I don't think mentioning him has ever gotten that reaction," Melissa laughs.

"What she means is Critter is a legend with us," Cassie says. "He's the only person alive that we can't track. At least not for long. He may not see us, but eventually he gets spooked and ditches us. He's good."

"Really good," Brittany adds.

"I spent a whole day trying to find him once," Lacy agrees, "lost him after fifteen minutes and never found him again."

"Yeah, that's my Uncle Critter," Melissa says. "Slipperier than squirrel shit."

This sends the women into a laughing fit and it's a few minutes before the giggles finally die down.

"Squirrel shit," Brittany snickers.

The light starts to dwindle through the massive windows behind us and I realize it must be close to eight at night. Jesus, Stella must be freaking out! I pull out my phone and try to text her, but it doesn't go through.

"Your phone work?" I ask Stuart.

He tries his again and again then shakes his head. Melissa's is out too. So is the PC's (Jeff. Apparently, the guy's name is Jeff. Need to remember that).

"Wi-Fi is out," Cassie says. "Started going down as soon as the mega-herd moved past the power plant and up I-26. By the time the Zs hit I-40 it was out city wide."

"How do you know that?" Stuart asks.

Cassie pulls out her own phone. "We've been monitoring all communications for months." She shrugs. "Seemed like a good idea."

"That's how you know so much about my family," I say. Cassie smiles and nods.

"I have to pee," Elsbeth says. Or Carly. No, no, she's Elsbeth.

"Pee outside," Stacy says. "The toilets are tricky in this house. We only use them during winter when we have to. Keeps the plumbing issues down."

"So you have running water?" I ask as Elsbeth gets up and walks quickly from the room.

"Yep," Brittany says. "There's a huge cistern on the grounds. And we have rain barrels. The water is gravity fed from tanks up top. It was the easiest way to hook it all up. Not all sinks work, of course. That would be too much."

"But the ones we need to work do," Cassie says.

"Cool," I say. Elsbeth still isn't back. "Um, I need to pee too."

Everyone smiles at me, but I can feel Cassie's eyes watching as I leave the room. I hurry outside in the direction I think Elsbeth

CHAPTER FOUR

"Get them in the gate!" Stella screams as she hurries past the lines of wounded. "Move it! We have to get this closed, NOW!"

Her eyes go wide as she see's Big Daddy Fitzpatrick being carried into Whispering Pines, half his face a torn mess and his clothes scorched and smoking. Her hand goes to her mouth, but she fights the gorge that wants to rise.

Shit needs to get done and Stella gets shit done.

"Buzz!" she yells as she sees one of Big Daddy's sons help push people from Highway 251 and into Whispering Pines. "BUZZ!"

"Holy shit, Stella," he says as he runs up to her, "they're everywhere!"

"What is going on?"

"Zs," he says, "herds of them."

"Herds…?" She lets the plural sink in. "But…how?"

"We don't know the how, ma'am," Critter says as he joins them after shouting orders to his crew. "But we know the numbers." He glances at Buzz. "You want to tell her?"

"Thousands," he says, "maybe tens of thousands."

"Mom? Mom!" Charlie yells from behind. "The Wi-Fi is down! We can't communicate with the Grove Park!"

"Shit," Stella says, wiping a blood-coated hand across her brow. "What the fuck is happening?"

"We're under attack," Critter says. "My guess? The powers that be are sick of our little rebuild effort. They are clearing the area of the living."

"Powers that be?" Stella asks. "You mean the Consortium?"

Critter shrugs, his bony shoulders nearly touching his ears. "Just a guess from my gut."

"I trust your gut," Buzz says.

"Me too," Stella says. She can see the way Buzz keeps looking around. "Your father? He's being hurried up to the infirmary. How'd he get burned?"

"Truck flipped," Buzz says, tears welling in his eyes. "My fault. We came around a bend and they were just there. A wall of Zs. I tried to keep control, but we went into a ditch and then it was all downhill from there."

"Literally," Critter adds. "I watched them roll a hundred feet."

"We lost the Fertigs, the Santiagos," Buzz says, "the Patels, and they were going to move into the Grove Park so the girls could take advantage of the school being set up there."

"The Patels?" Stella gasps. "Jennifer too?" Buzz nods. "Oh, God…Charlie…"

She spins and sees her son standing there. His face is ashen and his jaw hangs open as he slowly shakes his head. Jennifer Patel. His girlfriend.

"You're wrong," he growls, his eyes on Buzz, "they weren't moving until tomorrow. She said so last night."

"Sorry, bud," Buzz says, "they decided to train over with everyone going to the Counsel meeting. More room to haul their stuff that way."

"No. No!" Charlie snaps. "NO! FUCK YOU, BUZZ!"

He leaps at the man, his seventeen year old teenage body slamming into the farm bred brick house that is Buzz Fitzpatrick. Buzz takes it in stride, let's Charlie slam his fists against him over and over until the boy is exhausted and ready to collapse. Buzz takes him in his arms and holds him tight, his eyes filled with tears for the pain he feels. For the pain they all feel.

"I know, I know," Buzz says, "I'm sorry."

Stella has her hands to her mouth, her eyes wide with fear.

"Where's your man?" Critter asks then stops. "Wait…what're *you* doin' here, boss lady? Why ain't you at the Grove Park for the meeting?"

"My stomach wasn't feeling well," she answers, "Jace went for me."

"Shit," Critter says, "then he's out there and not here."

"He's out there," Stella says, stunned with the reality of that statement, "with the Zs."

Pup and Porky, the Fitzpatrick twins that are easily as big as their older brother is, come running up to them.

"We can't get the Farm," Pup says.

"Wi-Fi won't work," Porky adds.

"How the hell is it out everywhere?" Critter asks, rubbing the grizzled stubble on his head. "It was working this morning."

"We didn't have herds of Zs this morning," Buzz says.

Charlie pushes away and wipes his eyes. "Cutting off enemy communications is step one in a major attack. Then cut off supplies and if possible, overwhelm with numbers."

"I'd say it's more than possible," Critter says. "Sheee-it. This is fucking war."

"And the soldiers are at the Grove Park," Buzz says, "right?"

Stella nods. "There's some PCs here, but Lourdes is at the GPI. And we can't call her."

***

"I want a status report!" Lourdes Torres shouts as she slams her hand down on the table. "Somebody tell me something!"

"We can't," one of the PCs, Hermes "Shots" Leonides says, "com is down. Radio is static. Wi-Fi is nothing. We are dead in the water."

Lourdes rubs her face and looks at her command team. "As of right now we will consider this an all out attack. Asheville is under siege. I want all assault Teams geared up and ready in ten minutes. Pack for the field because once we leave here we may not be back for a while."

"Jesus," Barbara "Babs" Carlyle says, "this is fucking Cleveland all over again."

"Hardly," Sean "Poker Face" Booker replies. "Don't smell half as bad as Cleveland."

"Ten minutes," Lourdes says. "Go!"

***

The body armor protects his forearm as the Z chomps down, but Joe T still cries out, more from rage than pain. He swings his arm, lifting the Z like a terrier hanging onto a chew toy, and flings the thing halfway across the water transfer station.

Men and women scream about him, whether because they are fighting for their lives or losing their lives, Joe T can't tell. All he knows is everything has gone to shit in a fucking hand basket in seconds. His instincts tell him to abandon the station and get his ass back to base, back to the Grove Park, but his duty tells him he has to fight and fight and fight until he kills every last Z or is killed by them.

"Joe!" a man yells close by. "I'm out! I need ammo!"

Joe T has one magazine left for his M-4 and tosses it to the man, letting his rifle drop as he pulls his Desert Eagle from his hip. He fires once and vaporizes a Z's skull as it lurches towards him. He fires again, ripping the top half of a Z's head off. He fires a third time, but only nails a Z's chest as the things get too close to get a good shot off. Joe T is about to go down under a pile of the undead.

"Fall back!" Joe T yells. "Get the fuck out of here!"

He runs backward, firing until his pistol clicks empty. A quick glance over his shoulder tells him he's close to where he wants to be and that's by the main valve system.

"Let's purge," he scowls.

He bashes a Z over the head with his empty pistol, crushing the thing's skull. Kicking out, he knocks another Z against the ever encroaching herd. It gives him enough time to hop up onto a metal platform and turn his attention to a large valve prominently painted red. The warning sign by the valve reads, "Danger. Do not open fully. High pressure. Do not open fully. Danger."

"Let's schedule some maintenance," Joe T says. "HEADS UP!"

Those men and women still alive glance his way, see what he's about to do, and book it to higher ground. They jump up on vehicles, climb utility poles, scramble on top of the trailer used as an office. They all get anywhere that isn't the ground.

Joe T twists the valve with all his might. It doesn't move. He braces his legs and readjusts his grip. His muscles strain, tendons in his neck close to snapping, as he cranks, and cranks, and cranks. Finally, the valve starts to ease. He turns as fast as he can and a loud warning claxon rings out across the station.

Joe T steps back, grabs a fresh magazine, ejects the spent one from his Desert Eagle, and slams the fresh one home. The Zs surround his little platform, their hungry faces looking up at him, their arms outstretched, needing, wanting, yearning.

"Hungry, fuckers?" Joe T asks. "Too bad because all we got is drinks tonight."

There's a groaning within the complex of pipes and Joe T smiles down at the undead herd.

Then everything bursts around him, enveloping his body in an explosion of water and iron.

***

"I want all bitten in the house next door!" Dr. McCormick shouts. "I don't care what their other wounds are! The infirmary is for people I can fucking save, not for the already dead!"

"We can't just leave them to die," Greta Stanford snaps. Fourteen years old, she is a tall, long legged mix of her mother and father. "They need help!"

"There's nothing I can help them with!" Dr. McCormick snaps. "A bite is death!"

"My dad was bitten and he cut off his own arm! We can help them!" Greta says.

A woman screams as she is dragged into the infirmary, clutching at her stomach as her intestines spill from between her fingers. A man wails as he stares at what used to be his hands, but are now mangled twists of bone and flesh.

Dr. McCormick looks around and realizes what she's seeing and it's like a veil has been lifted.

They've all been bitten.

She turns to Greta. "I need every saw we have. I want blowtorches, propane stoves, anything that can cauterize a wound. Get me axes, machetes, whatever I can start hacking with. And I need more people! We'll start at this end and work down. Someone hacks and someone burns. Got it?"

"Got it," Greta nods as she runs from the infirmary.

"Sweet, God, help me," Dr. McCormick whispers, "God help us all."

***

"Close it up!" Stella yells. "Close the gates!"

She stands at the top of the watchtower next to the massive gate that marks the entrance to Whispering Pines. The wounded keep coming, most of them clutching others that are in even worse shape than they are. She knows that if she closes the gates she'll strand dozens outside. But she has no choice.

The Zs are right behind them. She can see hundreds coming, shuffling and moaning their way to the buffet on legs.

She has no choice.

***

"AAAAAAAAAHHHH!" a man screams as Greta hacks off his leg at the knee.

"Burn that!" she yells to the woman standing next to her with a hand held butane torch. "Don't fucking stand there! Close that wound!"

"But I...I can't," the woman says.

Greta grabs the torch from the woman and presses the blue flame against the man's leg. He screams again then passes out.

"Fuck you," Greta says to the woman, "get your useless fucking ass away from me."

Hatchet in one hand, torch in the other, Greta moves to the next man. He looks from the hatchet to the torch as he clutches his wrist.

"Take the whole arm," he grunts, "only way to be sure."

is almost sucked from his lungs. He's up and sprinting towards the chaos before the last explosion has left his ears.

Through the haze, he sees shapes moving forward.

"Headshots! HEADSHOTS!" he screams. "Make it count, motherfuckers!"

***

"What do you mean?" Buzz asks as he stands next to the cot draped with a bloody sheet. "He can't be gone."

"He wasn't a young man anymore," Dr. McCormick says. "The shock of his wounds was too much for his heart to take. I'm sorry."

"Oh, Lord," Buzz says, "what now?"

"I don't know," Dr. McCormick says as she hurries away.

"But the Farm?" Buzz mumbles. "I can't run that by myself. I can't."

"BUZZ!" Charlie yells as he runs into the infirmary. "We need you down at the gate! It may not hold!"

"Yeah, yeah," Buzz says.

Charlie catches sight of the cot and frowns. "That's not..."

"Yeah, it is," Buzz says.

"This day sucks dick," Charlie says.

"Yep," Buzz says as he turns from his father's covered corpse. "Let's go."

***

"Mother of God, where did they come from?" The driver asks as Lourdes stands by the railing of the Elk Mountian Rd overpass, her scope to her eye as she studies the herd of Zs that pushes past the abandoned cars and trucks on I-26.

"South, obviously," Lourdes says, watching Zs stumble up and down off/on ramps, spilling into the neighborhoods like a virus spreading through arteries. "We need to move."

"You think Whispering Pines will hold?" the driver asks.

"I don't know," Lourdes replies, "maybe. They might have a chance if the zeds don't make it all the way to them. They might disperse enough that we can manage a few waves."

"We?"

"Yeah, we," Lourdes says as she comes around and hops back into the Humvee. She reaches out the window and gives a thumbs up to the convoy of six Humvees behind her. "Get us there fast."

The driver nods and punches the accelerator. They twist and turn their way down Elk Mountain Rd until they hit Hwy 251. He turns the Humvee left, but slows the vehicle after going only a hundred yards or so. They crest a small hill and see the nightmare before them.

"Back," Lourdes says.

"But we can cut up 6th Ave and sneak in the back way," the driver says. "I can take this left here."

"Too late," Lourdes says. "Back. We'll double around to the cliff. Go in that way."

"But..."

"Do it!" Lourdes yells, pointing out the windshield. "We'll have high ground. We go up 6th and we'll be trapped there in minutes! Look at them all!"

The mass of Zs before them groan and hiss. Many of them scrape at the hillside, knowing there is food in Whispering Pines if they can just get to it. A few turn and spot the Humvee convoy. They bare their teeth and start forward.

"See," Lourdes says, suddenly very, very tired. "Go."

The driver reaches out the window and twirls his arm about. The Humvees all start to turn around then pull to the side to let Lourdes's vehicle take the lead once more. Back up Elk Mountain Rd they go. They turn onto Jonestown Rd and speed through the twists of the small, residential street.

"There," Lourdes says as they come to an unassuming ranch house.

The convoy stops and PCs instantly hop out, rifles ready, eyes on their surroundings. Lourdes does a head count.

"Vehicles one through three stay," she says, "the rest head back to the Grove Park. Evacuate the place. Anyone that doesn't want to go can rot."

"Where to?" a PC asks.

"Take them to Reynolds Mountain," Lourdes says, "it'll give you the higher ground. Dig in. I want gun nests every twenty yards. If we can't hold Whispering Pines then we'll be coming your way. Be ready."

The PCs nod and hop back into Humvees four through six. Lourdes watches them speed off then turns and starts hiking towards the field that connects with the back cliff that Phase One of Whispering Pines butts up against. She plans on finding out their status and then making the call from there.

"I'm going in," Lourdes says to her people. "I want you all to scour the area for vehicles that will run. The bigger the better. Bring them back here and secure the area. If we need to evacuate Whispering Pines then we'll be coming fast. Jonestown Rd connects to Riverside down below, which connects to I-26 back near Broadway. We may not have much time before the Zs figure that out."

***

"To the cliff!" Stella shouts.

"Mom!" Greta screams as she sprints towards the watchtower. "Dr. McCormick won't come with! She says she's staying with the wounded!"

"Like hell she is!" Stella growls. She climbs down from the watchtower, the ever present roar of the Zs at the gate grating on her last, frayed nerve.

Stella sprints up and down the hills of Whispering Pines until she gets to the infirmary. Out of breath, adrenaline pumping through her, she bursts in, spots Dr. McCormick and grabs the woman by the arm.

"Hey!" Dr. McCormick yells. "OW! Stella, stop!"

"We get everyone out that we can," Stella says, "and that includes you."

"I have thirty people dying here," Dr. McCormick says, "I'm not leaving them alone. I'm not."

"Reaper is off with Platt and John," Stella says, "that means you are our only trained medical professional. We have fifty plus men, women, and children that will need your help if shit goes wrong. Which it will. I can guarantee that."

"Stella, listen…"

"You are coming!" Stella roars. "Do what you can for whomever you can. Get those that can move ready. We are evacuating to the cliff."

"The cliff?" Dr. McCormick laughs. "Now I know you've lost your mind. We'll never get half these people up those stairs, let alone maneuver them through the razor wire, fencing, and ditches."

"Then half stay," Stella states as she turns and hurries from the room.

Greta stands there, her mouth wide open.

"Is it that bad?" Dr. McCormick asks. "Are the gates coming down?"

Greta can't speak so she just nods.

"Fine," Dr. McCormick says. "Grab me a marker. I'll tag those I think can move on their own. Everyone else will need help. We leave no one if we don't have to."

***

When Lourdes gets to the bottom of the cliff stairs and sees the groups of Whispering Pines residents hurrying towards her, she knows the shit has hit it and it's all a fucking mess.

"Where's Stella Stanford?" Lourdes asks a resident.

"She was down by the gates," the woman says, holding a toddler to her chest. "But someone said she may be at the infirmary."

"What happened here?" Lourdes asks.

"The Zs," the woman says as she pushes past and hurries away.

"Nuff said," Lourdes mumbles. She readies her rifle as she hikes against the throng rushing to the cliff.

She gets to the bottom of the hill, where Phase One stops and the entrance to the subdivision begins. People are running everywhere and it's complete chaos. She can hear the moans of the Zs and the sounds of their putrid hands smacking against the thick wood of the front gates.

"He will wipe every tear from their eyes. There will be no more death or mourning or crying or pain, for the old order of things has passed away," a raspy voice says off to her side. "Revelation 21:4."

Lourdes turns to see Preacher Carrey standing there, his white hair a wild tangle about his head, his eyes rolling, rolling, rolling madly in his skull.

"Whatever," Lourdes says as she sees Stella running back towards the gates.

She hurries down and intercepts the woman.

"How long will the gates hold?" she asks Stella.

"What? Lourdes? When did you get here?" Stella asks, her arms waving madly, directing people from Phase Two and up into Phase One. "How many are with you?"

"I have fifteen up on Jonestown Rd looking for vehicles," Lourdes replies, "looks like we'll need them."

"Good, good," Stella says. "I kept meaning to have some up there ready, but we've just been so busy rebuilding." Stella stops and looks around. Her chest hitches and she starts to breathe quickly.

"Whoa, whoa, whoa," Lourdes says, "sit down."

"Can't...breathe," Stella says.

"You're hyperventilating," Lourdes replies as she helps Stella to the curb. "Put your head between your legs and take some deep breaths."

"It's just...so...sudden," Stella says.

"Hush. Calm, even breaths."

It takes Stella a second, but she gets it under control.

"I don't know where Jace is," Stella says, looking Lourdes in the eye. "I don't even know where my kids are. I've told them to help with so many things I can't remember what I said last."

"First, I'm sure Jace is fine," Lourdes says, "he's a wily bastard." This gets a small smile from Stella. "Second, I'll handle things down here. You go find your kids."

"I don't know where to start," Stella says.

"My nephews'll help," Critter says as he comes up and crouches down next to Stella. "They'll go with ya. I'll help the lady soldier get your folk up and out."

84

Stella looks up and sees Pup and Porky standing there.

"I'm sorry about your father," she says.

"About what?" Critter asks. "What happened?"

"Oh," Stella replies, "Hollis died. I thought Buzz would have told you."

Critter sighs. "Haven't seen him for a while," he says, "but I'm not surprised. Shit's crazy wild 'round here. Ain't surprised 'bout Hollis, neither. He was hurt bad."

"Mom!" Charlie yells. "Mom!"

"See, boss lady, I found one of them for ya already," Critter smiles. It's a smile that doesn't reach his sad eyes. "Now we just have to find one more."

"Greta's still with Dr. McCormick," Charlie says.

"Right, of course," Stella nods.

"Hey," Buzz says as he comes up behind Charlie.

"It true, bro?" Pup asks.

"Daddy dead?" Porky follows.

"Yep," Buzz nods. "Nothing the doctor could do." He looks around. "Where you want me? At the gate?"

"No point," Stella says as a loud crack echoes through the air, "it won't hold. We're getting out by the cliff. Can you and your brothers go get the vans up at the Church? They'll need them back at the infirmary. And tell Dr. McCormick I'm sorry for being such a bitch. No, never mind. I'll tell her myself. I have to go back and get Greta. You just get the vans. God, I'm tired."

Buzz nods at Stella then nods to his brothers. The men quickly walk up the hill towards the Church of Jesus of the Light. Critter stands and watches his nephews go.

"They're good boys," Critter says. "But nothing will replace their daddy. Don't know how the Farm will keep going."

"We need to worry about other things now," Lourdes says. "Critter, can you walk Stella to the infirmary? I'm going to check on the gates and see how much time we have then keep the evacuation going."

"Yes, ma'am," Critter says as he helps Stella stand.

"What about me?" Charlie asks. "What do I do?"

"You stay by my side," Stella says, "and don't leave my sight." She looks around the subdivision. "We could sure use Sergeant

85

Platt right now. He'd be barking orders left and right, keeping things in line."

"I don't bark," Lourdes says, "but I do bite. Maybe that'll move some of the stragglers along."

***

The baton spears the Z's head and after a couple of stuttered hisses the monster stills.

"They're getting thick again," Weapons Sergeant Sammy "John" Baptiste says as he pulls the baton out and flicks the red-black goop from it. "I thought we'd gotten through the worst."

"It's like a storm," Medical Sergeant Alex "Reaper" Stillwater says, coming up next to John, wiping his own baton. "We're hitting waves of the things."

"That means what's behind us isn't the first wave," Master Sergeant Joshua Platt adds as he shoves two Zs off of himself and gets to his feet, a gore covered knife in his hand. "They're attacking now. Dammit."

"Radio is dead," John says. "Can't even pick up short wave."

"They have jammers already in place," Platt says. "We're too late. They've been planning this for a long time. I think we just upped their time table." He pats the heavy pack on his back. "Hopefully this is all they had."

"You think so?" John asks, not buying it.

"I don't," Platt says, "or it wouldn't have been so easy to get."

"Easy?" Reaper laughs, pointing to his bruised and cut face.

"We're still alive, correct?" Platt asks. "Pull your panties out of your ass."

"Yes, sir," Reaper sneers.

"There should be one of Critter's caches up ahead," John says as he checks his compass. "Just over that ridge."

The three Special Forces soldiers, what's left of the elite ODA Team Cobra out of Fort Bragg, NC, begin yet another leg of their journey from Atlanta, GA. They'd left Asheville weeks ago, determined to get intel on what the group known as the Consortium was up to in good ol' Hotlanta.

They found the intel they needed, which did not bode well for the residents of Asheville trying to put the pieces back together. And they found something else. Something they carry with them as they hurry to get back to the people they have sworn to protect.

If they can get past the thousands of Zs that choke I-26, spilling off into the side highways and environment beyond, that is.

They dodge a few rogue groups of Zs, choosing to evade instead of engage and possibly draw attention, and crest the ridge. They instantly hit the dirt, flattening themselves against the ridge line, hoping they haven't already been spotted.

"Those aren't Zs," John says. He unslings his sniper rifle and puts it to his shoulder, his eye looking through the scope. One hundred mile per hour tape covers part of the front lens, keeping any sun flare on the scope from giving away their position. "I count, four, five, six men. Well armed, all watching the Zs carefully."

"What the hell?" Reaper says. "Since when did Zs need chaperones?"

"Since they need to be herded in a specific direction," Platt replies.

"So, what, they're shepherds? Wranglers? Ranchers?" Reaper asks. "Jesus."

"I can see black gunk smeared all over their clothes," John says. "They're using Z guts as sensory camouflage. Same as the security patrols in Atlanta."

"Can we get down the ridge without them seeing?" Platt asks.

The Atlanta men are all standing on a high bridge spanning the French Broad River. The river flows down below the Z covered bridge as well as the ridge Platt and his men are perched on. John watches the men closely, gauging their attention to their surroundings coupled with the distance from the bridge to the ridge.

"Yeah," John says, "they're occupied with the Zs. With the gear they have, and the numbers of Zs they have, I doubt they're worried about much other than staying stinky and keeping themselves from being eaten."

"Good," Platt nods, "we're about to lose the sun. We need to get to the cache and down to the river as soon as the light is gone. We don't have time to wait."

John slings his rifle and slides after Platt and Reaper as they carefully navigate the hillside on the other side of the ridge. They get to a barely visible deer trail and silently make their way to a small outcropping of granite. John crawls underneath and then gives a short whistle as he shoves a good amount of deadfall towards Reaper and Platt.

The two men get down and crawl in behind John. Both are pleasantly surprised that they can stand up fully after only crawling a couple feet.

"Nice," Reaper says. "Are those cots? Man, I could sleep for a year."

"We all could," Platt says, "But…"

"It's not going to happen," Reaper nods, "I know. Just dreaming."

"Rafts," Platt says. "Find those first. Then ammo, food, and water."

"Water's right here," John says, tossing a bottle to Platt. "Looks like only a few MREs for food."

"What flavors?" Reaper asks.

"Chicken lasagna," John says.

"Pass," Platt and Reaper say at the same time.

"Is it chicken lasagna that makes you crap so bad it comes out your pores?" John asks. Reaper nods. "Right. I'll pass also."

They stack three large, rubber cubes by the cache entrance then go back to add to their dwindling ammo.

"No magazines for my rifle," John sighs. "I was worried about that."

"How many rounds do you have?" Platt asks.

"Four full magazines," John replies. "But I get twitchy when I have less than eight."

"Understood," Platt nods. "If you men are set then let's move out."

They gear up and exit the cache one at a time. John covers the entrance and let's Reaper then Platt slide past him as he watches the men on the bridge with his scope. He waits as Platt and Reaper get all the way down to the riverbank before he slings his rifle and slides down after them.

A small copse of oaks give them enough cover to pull the tab and let one of the cubes auto-inflate into a six person raft. The hissing sound of air being sucked into the raft makes them all nervous, but John keeps his eye on the men up above. None seem to notice. It would take a lot to divert one's attention from a massive herd of Zs.

They toss in the other two cubes and their packs, along with the heavy pack Platt has kept with him since Atlanta. Reaper starts to shove the raft off as Platt gets in then follows. John waits until the last possible second and tumbles into the raft, coming up on his belly with his rifle resting on the side of the raft, aimed at the men on the bridge.

The raft drifts along the shallows for several yards before coming to a bend in the French Broad. Once the bridge is out of sight, John takes a deep breath and rolls onto his back.

"It's 1930 right now," Platt says, looking at his watch. "It'll be close to 0400 before we get to the landing by Whispering Pines. You two grab some shuteye. I'll keep an eye on the banks and wake John at 2130. Reaper, you have watch at 0100. Understood?"

"Understood," Reaper says as he settles into the bottom of the raft.

"Got it," John replies as he does the same.

It takes them both less than a minute to be sound asleep. As a Special Forces soldier you learn to sleep when you can, wherever you can.

Platt watches the ripples in the dark green water as his thoughts drift to the past few weeks of action.

The three of them set out to get some intel on the Consortium's operations in Atlanta. Knowing what they were up against was the only way to know if they stood a chance. Sadly, what they found confirmed what he'd feared: they do not stand a chance.

Atlanta is surrounded by herd after herd after herd of Zs and all carefully contained and managed by several dozen armed keepers. Platt could easily tell the men and women weren't military professionals, but they were tough and looked like they knew how to handle themselves in a fight. His guess? They cut their teeth in

Atlanta's deadly crime underground before Z-Day hit. After Z-Day, the weak were thinned out, just like everywhere else, leaving only those that would do anything they could to survive. And joining up with the Consortium was a good way to survive.

It took them a week of scouting just to find a weak point so they could get into Atlanta proper. What they found was not what Platt expected. He figured things would be organized, but would also look like a scene from the Road Warrior: desperate groups all co-mingling in order to stay alive just a few more days. That wasn't the case.

Atlanta, at least the parts that were occupied and developed, was clean, orderly, and the picture of post-apocalyptic efficiency. Running water, solar and wind energy, neighborhood gardens and markets, even trash pickup in large, horse drawn carts. People seemed happy, people seemed content, people seemed satisfied with their lives.

But Platt was trained to look below the surface smiles and fake laughs. It didn't take them long to discover that the order and efficiency was brutally enforced. Within a day, they saw their first public executions and by the end of the first week, they'd witnessed an entire family lynched because they were growing food in a spare bedroom without permission.

It took all his self-control and discipline to keep from gunning down the "security" men that tightened the nooses. He doubts he'll ever get the faces of those children out of his mind.

By week three, they had been able to infiltrate a group of single men that stayed close to mid-town. A few bribes with some canned goods and pints of scotch they'd picked up on the trip down and they were given ID badges and assigned work duties, no questions asked. By the end of the fourth week, Reaper had gotten himself a position within the main medical center.

From there they learned that Atlanta was well aware of what was going on in Asheville and none too pleased with it. Officials from the Consortium spent a good amount of time in the medical center, keeping up with the constant breakouts of various diseases that occur when you pack a large population together while also controlling their food and water rations. Even despite the trash pickup, and running water, people were still undernourished and basic preventive medications and vaccines were completely depleted.

John was able to get in with the security team, which gave him access to the munitions dumps, various armories, and security barracks set up throughout the city. In days he had intel that Atlanta was planning a full on siege of Asheville. The only thing in Asheville's favor, it seemed, was Atlanta's overconfidence. There were plenty of loose lips ready to sink ships.

Even with all of the information they gathered, there wasn't a sense of urgency until John came back to the small apartment the men shared with four others and dropped a bomb. A very dirty bomb.

"They have uranium," John had whispered one night, "and they plan on using it."

A dirty bomb, explosives wrapped about uranium that would explode and spread deadly radioactive materials for miles, was one way to kill Asheville. So Platt came up with a plan to relieve Atlanta of its dirty, little secret. It took them another two weeks to put the plan into place.

When the night came, the three men quickly figured out they weren't as covert as they had thought. A security team was waiting for them. Unfortunately for those men, they didn't have the SpecOps training that Platt, Reaper, and John did. It wasn't an easy fight, but they were able to get the C4 encased uranium and get the hell out of Hotlanta.

But, as they found out, Atlanta had more than one trick up its sleeve.

And Platt can hear that trick moaning and groaning hundreds of feet up above the river.

Tired of running everything through his head, he stretches out in the raft and watches the tops of the trees sway in the evening breeze. He can't see the interstate above, but the constant sounds of the Zs make it clear it isn't too far off. If his memory serves him, they have quite a few miles of cover before they float back into sight of the highway. But by that time, it will be dark and the last thing the Z wranglers will be looking for is a raft floating the French Broad.

Or so he thinks.

The first flicker of light Platt sees near the shore he chalks up to a reflection from the endless amounts of mica rock that the Blue Ridge Mountains are made up of. The second flicker, only a few yards past the first one, makes him take notice. It is too uniform, too much of a coincidence, too similar to the flare off a scope.

"John, Reaper," Platt whispers as he taps them with his boots, "Company."

The men are trained professionals and they only open their eyes and neither moving a muscle to give away that they are awake and alert.

"Numbers?" John asks.

"At least two," Platt says as he eases the barrel of his rifle up onto the side of the raft. "But let's assume there's more."

Platt lets out a quiet laugh as he glances down at John. The hope is that it makes him look like he is casually joking around and not scanning the surroundings out of the corner of his eye. It is obvious the rouse doesn't work when a loud cough is accompanied by the sound of a bullet whizzing past Platt's ear.

"Fuck," Platt snaps, "suppressors. We're in the shit, boys!"

Both Reaper and John roll up to the side of the raft, their rifles ready, but they hold their fire.

"Where am I looking?" John asks.

"Two o'clock and about ten yards down from that," Platt says, his finger on the trigger, ready to return fire. He has no plans just to start shooting, not until he knows for certain where the targets are.

John dials in his scope and watches the tree line by the riverbank. "Got one," he says.

"Take him," Platt orders.

John squeezes the trigger and his rifle barks. A man cries out and then all the shit hits all the fans at once.

Bullets from at least six automatic rifles tear up low hanging branches and vines along the riverside. The water is puckered by slugs as the shooters begin gauging the distance from shore to raft. John answers the gunfire, taking careful aim as he sights on the various muzzle flashes that come from the shadows of the riverbank.

Platt and Reaper don't bother with John's finesse and let loose with their M-4s. More men cry out, but the gunfire doesn't slacken, telling the men that there are more than just six shooters.

The raft hisses once then twice as it is punctured by gunfire. Platt calculates that they have about ten minutes before they take on water and have to swim for it. When a third hiss starts, he tosses all calculations out the window and concentrates on his return fire. Which lasts all of eight seconds before two slugs rip into him.

"Fuck!" he shouts as pain explodes in his left shoulder and then deep into his chest. He keeps firing for as long as he can before the wounds force him to let go of his rifle and slide down to the bottom of the raft.

"Sergeant?" Reaper shouts. "What's your status?"

"Left shoulder…is ground meat," Platt says as he struggles for breath. "Also pretty sure…a…slug entered through my…shoulder and hit…my left…lung."

"Fucking fuck shit," John says. "They're moving back into the shadows too far. I'm losing them."

He nails three more men before he rolls and ducks down into the raft with Platt. Reaper joins them and they cover their heads as bullets continue to puncture the raft again and again.

"Sergeant?" Reaper asks. "Talk to me."

"No," Platt gasps. "Hurts…too…much."

"Good," Reaper says, "that means you're still alive. Focus on that pain. FUCK!"

He clamps a hand to his ear then pulls it back to see the palm covered in blood.

"Fucker took off the top of your ear!" John shouts. He grabs Reaper's M-4 and pops up, emptying the magazine at the riverbank. "FUCK OFF!"

He can hear the bullets, and feel their heat, but none of the enemy slugs hit home. By the time he's emptied a second magazine the gunfire from the tree line stops. The damaged raft floats around a wide curve and the landscape changes as the river cuts through a large ravine. John listens closely, but can't hear the sound of Zs anymore.

"We've pulled away from the interstate," he says. "I don't think they can follow us for now. The sides are too steep."

"Get us to shore," Reaper says, his hands pressing a pack of gauze against Platt's shoulder. "I need space to work and we need a new raft."

John grabs the small paddle and steers them to the side of the ravine. As soon as the riverbank turns back to mud and sand instead of sheer rock, he paddles them over and hops out, pulling them up onto shore.

Reaper slices Platt's shirt off and studies the wounds. Platt's clavicle is shattered, that's easy to see, but the other wound, the deeper one that's in his chest, is near impossible for Reaper to work on.

"I'm going to have to open him up," Reaper says. "Hold pressure here."

John switches places with Reaper as the medic digs through his pack for his med kit. He pulls out s stethoscope and places it to Platt's chest. It takes him a few seconds of searching before he hears the gurgling deep in Platt's left lung.

"Jesus," Reaper says. "I don't know if I can get to it. The entry wound is from above, not through the front. I'd have to open his chest and crack his ribs to extract the bullet."

"And that's not happening from the side of the French Broad," John says. "What now?"

Reaper pulls out a scalpel, some iodine, and a short, plastic tube.

"I insert this and keep his lung from filling up with blood," Reaper says. "While you get another raft ready. His only chance is to get him back to Whispering Pines and Dr. McCormick. She has what we need in her infirmary."

"You think he'll live that long?" John asks.

"I can…hear you," Platt says, his eyes looking at Reaper. "But answer…the question."

"If I can drain your lung and you don't bleed out?" Reaper replies. "Yes, sir, I think you'll make it."

"Good," Platt nods. "Then start cutting. We wait until full dark before getting back on the river. We'll be lucky if they aren't searching for us."

***

"They've breached the hill in Phase Two!" someone screams. "Run! RUN!"

"Jesus," Dr. McCormick says, "we still have a dozen wounded in the infirmary."

"They're lost," Lourdes replies, pushing Dr. McCormick up the cliff stairs. "I need you to focus on the living."

"I can't just leave them!" Dr. McCormick shouts. "They'll die!"

"How many do you think will die without you around, Doc?" Lourdes shouts back. "All these people that rely on you every day? How many will make it a week, a month, a year without your expertise? You aren't going back! No one is!"

"You cold hearted bitch," Dr. McCormick snarls.

"Call me what you want, lady," Lourdes replies, "but you're a doctor, you should know better. Sometimes you have to make the tough calls even if they suck. That's why they're tough."

"I was a proctologist," Dr. McCormick mutters.

"What's that?"

"I fixed assholes!" Dr. McCormick yells. "I wasn't an ER doctor or heart surgeon! The toughest call I had to make was what steroidal hemorrhoid cream to prescribe!"

Lourdes shakes her head, but can't help smiling. Even with all the destruction and death around her. You take it where you can.

"Get going, Doc," Lourdes says, "I'm not telling you again."

Screams from down the hill make everyone stop for a second prompting Lourdes to start yelling and screaming at them to move. Most do, but some at the top are frozen in place, the view allowing them to see what's coming for everyone.

Zs. Hundreds of Zs.

Lourdes gets to the top and turns as she shoves people up into the field. Her jaw doesn't drop, she's too much of a pro for that, but her heart gives a little skip and she can feel her adrenaline kick up a notch.

"They must have piled up on the fencing and razor wire," one of her PCs says. "They just overwhelmed everything."

"How many are still in the subdivision?" Lourdes asks. "How many residents?"

"Hard to say," the man replies. "Never had an accurate count to begin with."

"There have to be a couple dozen," Stella says as she comes up to Lourdes, "maybe more."

"Shit," Lourdes says, glancing at Stella, "they'll never make it."

"Make it?" Stella says. "They have time. They can get up here."

Lourdes pulls two grenades from her vest; the PC does the same. Stella stares.

"No," she says. "Lourdes? What are you doing?"

"We have to blow the stairs or the zeds will follow us," Lourdes replies. "We don't have enough vehicles as it is, Stella. Some of us will have to wait for more to pick us up or start hiking it out. We need time to do that."

"Oh, God...," Stella whispers, "you'll trap them in there."

The herd of Zs can be seen coming from Phase Two and into Phase One. What they thought were a few hundred quickly turns into a thousand as the monsters crest the far off hill with no end in sight to their numbers.

"I don't want to do this," Lourdes says, "Jesus; I don't want to do any of this."

Stella nods, knowing that there are no easy answers in the zombie apocalypse. She leans across the railing and looks down at the residents still climbing the stairs.

"Hurry! All of you hurry!" she cries. "We're going to blow the stairs! Move, people! MOVE!"

Lourdes takes her gently by the arm. "Get to your kids. You don't need to see this. Get them in a Humvee."

"Where are we going?" Stella asks. "I heard that the route to the Grove Park Inn is cut off."

Lourdes looks at the PC and frowns. "I find out who's doing that chatting and their ass is mine." She looks at Stella. "I think we have only one option. And I doubt you'll like it."

"Why?" Stella asks then narrows her eyes. "No, I don't like it."

"No choice," Lourdes says. "They have the best defenses around. Now get. Go be with your kids. I'll join you in a minute."

"God," Stella says as she turns and runs through the field, making her way around the barricades and ditches as the sun sets over the hills. "Jace, where are you, baby? Where the fuck are you?"

CHAPTER FIVE

Pain to the left of me, agony to the right, stuck in the middle with FUCK!

I can't sleep. Stumpageddon is raising hell from all the fighting earlier and my shoulder is ten kinds of fucked. I need to get up and look at it, but I'm afraid to turn on a light and wake Stuart.

The sisters put us in one of the guest rooms on the second floor, one with a working toilet, albeit an ancient looking one, so I get up and tiptoe to the commode. I need to piss. But I look at the thing and think that with my luck I'll pull on the chain that hangs from the tank above and bring the whole thing crashing down. I tend to have shit luck with plumbing sometimes.

Ha, shit luck with plumbing. Funny.

So, downstairs I go. The Call of Nature will be answered outside as it was intended.

"Oh, hey," I say as I stop at the bottom of the stairs. "I didn't wake you up, did I?"

Cassie is standing there, stretching and rolling her head on her neck. She glances over and gives me an amused smile. "No, Long Pork, you didn't wake me. My shift is next so I'm limbering up first. Can't have cold, slow muscles when on the estate."

"Shift? What shift?" I ask.

"You aren't as smart as you think, are you?" she says.

"Just answer the question," I scowl, "and don't call me Long Pork. I hate that name."

"Do you? You don't seem to mind when Carly calls you that."

"Elsbeth," I correct, "she goes by Elsbeth."

"Her real name is Carly Michelle Thornberg," Cassie says.

"And my real name is Jason Stanford," I reply.

Cassie nods. "Fair enough. Jace, is it? That's the nickname you like?"

"Yeah, that's cool," I say. "So what's this shift? Security? I thought you ladies had the estate locked down pretty tight. Even if you don't, there's a lot of land to cover out there. Plus all the Zs staked in place. How can you even know if someone gets in?"

"The situation isn't perfect or foolproof," Cassie admits. "But you'd be surprised what you notice at night when you have to rely on other senses than your eyes. You'd also be surprised how many survivors think night is the time to go sightseeing. We detect more breaches between two and three in the morning than any other time."

"Survivors? Breaches?" I say. "What do you do with the survivors when you find them?"

Cassie gives me a cold look. "What we have to."

"Jesus..."

Cassie lets out a short laugh. "We don't kill them. Not right away, at least. Most we scare off by letting some of the Zs loose. The rest we take down and dump them outside the estate while they are unconscious."

"Why don't I think that's all you do?" I ask.

I cross my arm across my chest, but it doesn't have the same effect when half an arm is missing. Looks more like I'm comforting myself than trying to act tough and stern. Plus, my shoulder protests and I wince, which ruins everything quickly.

"You alright?" Cassie asks. "Were you wounded?"

"I'm fine, I'm fine," I say, "just sore from the day."

"You should stretch more," Cassie smiles.

"Thanks, Richard Simmons."

"Who?"

"Right," I smile, "I forget you're almost twenty years younger than me. Doesn't matter." I take a seat on the stairs as Cassie continues her stretches. "What does matter is the shit you told us earlier tonight. That's a pretty wild story. Kinda falls into the 'fantasy' realm of stories."

"If it was just me, I'd agree," Cassie says, "but you met the others, you spoke to them too. They confirmed it."

"Not the first time I've come across a brainwashed cult," I say. "You seem pretty persuasive. I wouldn't put it past you to be able to wrangle some other girls that are desperate for security and fill their heads with BS. Make them think they're special in some James Bond evil master plan way."

"Why would I do that?" Cassie asks. "Why go to all that trouble?"

"Why does anyone do anything these days?" I shrug. "Because you're bored, because you're crazy, because you're lonely."

"Do you actually believe any of the crap you're saying?" she asks.

"No," I reply quickly, "I believe what you said tonight. Knowing Elsbeth and what she can do, it makes sense. I always wondered how she was all Buffy skilled and shit. Plus, it fits with what Ms. Foster told me. The little that was."

"And?" she asks.

"And what?"

"And now what? Do you let Car- Elsbeth stay?" she asks.

"Let her...?" I laugh. "I don't *let* El do anything. She does what she wants and anyone that gets in her way is an idiot."

"Hmmm."

"Hmmm, what?"

"Oh, nothing, just back to that you not being as smart as you think you are thing."

"Out with it," I say. "I have to pee. I don't have time to wait for you to finish mocking me."

"She loves you," Cassie says, "any moron can see that."

"Whoa, whoa, whoa," I say, standing and holding up my hands. "I'm happily married. There's nothing between El and me."

"I know that," Cassie sighs. "I didn't mean she wants to fuck you and have babies. I meant that she loves you. You are obviously on her list of people she'd die for."

"Oh, right, that," I nod, "yeah, she's family. I'd die for her too. So would my kids. They love her."

"What about your wife? Would she die for Elsbeth?"

"If it came down to it, yes, I think she would," I answer. "Not like she'd die for our kids, but in the end she'd die for Elsbeth."

"Interesting," Cassie smiles. "I'm not so sure."

"I'm not either," I agree. "But knowing my wife, I think she would."

Cassie just keeps smiling then nods her head towards the huge main doors. "I thought you had to pee?"

"Right," I say, "I do. Thanks."

I walk to the doors and am almost outside when she speaks up.

"Oh, and Jace? When you come back, I'm having a look at that shoulder. That was a wounded wince, not a fatigued muscle wince. And all wounds get checked around here. Only way to be safe."

"Right, yeah sure," I say, my best fake smile planted on my face. "Only way to be safe."

I get outside and take a deep breath of the fresh air. But, it being the apocalypse and all, it's not as fresh as I'd like it to be. There's a hint of smoke and chemicals wafting by. And that ever present Eau de Zombie.

Instead of unzipping and letting it free right there, I hang a right and head towards the gardens. I have no intention of walking all the way down there, but I do want a little space between Cassie and me. The woman weirds me out. Gee, can't think why. Not like telling me that all those young women are heirs to some of the largest fortunes on the planet, and they also happen to be highly trained badasses that were brainwashed by a mad scientist, would be strange in any way. Nah, not strange at all.

But, like I said inside, it's the only thing that makes sense when it comes to Elsbeth. No normal canny girl could kill like she can. And, unfortunately, I've run into my share of cannies to know the difference.

I get down the stone steps and walk to the end of the vine covered trellis. I look out into the darkness at the huge field before me. Luckily, it's not populated with Zs. Only the outer fields are jammed with the unmoving undead. The wind blows across my face and I tilt my head, thinking I hear something. I wait. Nope. Nothing.

Pee pee time!

The relief of a good, long piss is one of the few simple pleasures left in life. Not trying to be crude, just stating a fact. With a shake and a zip I'm done.

Then I hear that sound again. What is that? It sounds like...footsteps! Coming fast!

I turn and sprint back towards the front doors, but barely get a few yards before I'm knocked on my ass.

"What the hell?" a woman's voice hisses. A blade is at my throat before I can answer. "Who are you?"

"Uh, it's me, Jace," I say. "Please don't, with the cutting of my throat."

"Oh, you," the woman says and the blade is gone. "Long Pork."

"My name is Jace, thank you," I say as she helps me up. "And you're...?"

"Marcie," she says. "Have you seen Cassie? Is she inside stretching?"

"I'm guessing that woman has a very set routine?"

"Shut up and answer the, Oh, forget it," Marcie says as she pushes me to the side and runs towards the front doors.

I follow after her as fast as I can, but running kills my shoulder. I need to look at the wound soon too before it gets worse. I'm praying it's not what I think it is. It can't be. Not now. Not after all this time.

I'm not even at the steps before the doors fly open and Cassie, along with four other women, burst out and rush past me.

"What the hell is going on?" I ask.

"Someone is down at the boat landing," Cassie says. "Soldiers. Marcie spotted their lights. Stay here while we deal with this."

Then they are gone, lost in the darkness that surrounds the house.

"Okay, see ya," I wave then turn and head back inside. "You guys can deal with the...soldiers?"

"What the hell is going on around here?" Stuart grumbles, pulling on a t-shirt over his muscled, scarred frame. "It sounded like a ninja girl stampede."

"Yeah, where'd they hurry off to?" Melissa asks from the stairs as she rubs the sleep from her eyes. "I finally got to sleep and then all hell breaks loose."

"Soldiers," I say, "down by the river."

"Soldiers?" Stuart asks then his eyes go wide as he comes to the same conclusion as I did. "Shit. We better get down there."

"Right," I nod, "you go after them. I'll wake up that PC guy....uh..."

"Jeff," Melissa says.

"Jeff! Yep, I'll wake up Jeff."

"You feeling okay, Jace?" Stuart asks me with his Master Gunnery Sergeant eyes boring into my suburban dad slash husband eyes.

"Fine," I say. "Never better. Just tired, is all."

Stuart looks back at Melissa. She shrugs.

"Okay, you get Jeff," Stuart says, "and bust ass, Stanford. We'll need your silver tongue to help smooth this out. I have a feeling the soldiers and the sisters may not get along."

"Come on," Melissa says as she grabs Stuart by the elbow and they hurry from the house.

I wait a minute before I turn and head towards one of the sitting rooms. I know there's a mirror in there.

It's pure agony as I struggle to get my t-shirt off. With only one hand, and a shoulder that feels like a trillion pieces of glass that are embedded in it, taking off a t-shirt goes from an everyday, ordinary task to a FUCKING KILL ME NOW task.

Not so fun.

Panting, drenched in sweat, I get the shirt off and let it fall to the ground as I stare at my reflection in the mirror. I'm really glad I already peed because my bladder spasms at the sight I see.

My shoulder is a mess. The skin is all kinds of browns and blues and yellows and blacks. The place where the fucking Z bit me looks like a whole lot of yuck. I can see the punctures in the skin and pus is oozing out. It seriously stinks.

I lean closer to the mirror, which isn't exactly perfectly clear. In fact, none of the mirrors are. I'm sure there are nice, modern mirrors somewhere in the residential floors that the Vanderbilt heirs lived in, but I don't have the time to go hunting for those rooms. Right now, I have to deal with the image in the antique glass in front of me.

That image shows me I'm fucked. And very alone.

I can't breathe a word of this to anybody. Not Stuart, not Melissa, not what's his name. And especially not Elsbeth.

Cassie may be right, that Elsbeth loves me like family, but I have a sinking feeling she wouldn't hesitate to put a blade through my eye socket if she thought I was infected.

Infected...

Fuck.

I can't be infected. I can't. Not after making it this far all these years. No, not after everything I've done. Being infected is not an option. There's Stella and the kids to think about and the rest of the people that rely on my big brain and me.

My big brain...

Time to dig deep and use that pile of grey matter. I haven't exactly been on my game lately. It's been months since I've had any burst of inspiration. I used to be the great generalist, the problem solver and the man with a plan.

But all I've really done since Stumpageddon took up permanent residence is go through the motions. Now, in my defense, learning to live with one hand does take a lot of ingenuity and brainpower. Brainpower I took for granted before.

Oh, who the fuck am I kidding? I'd lost my gift before that. The truth? After I blew up Whispering Pines and killed Vance, I sorta checked out. Not that anyone would notice. I kept up appearances by being the know it all dick I always was. It was that I just didn't have any new insights into the world around us anymore.

Now? I can't afford the luxury of a mental vacation. If I'm infected then I need to use my time as efficiently as possible.

I turn from the mirror and take a seat in one of the 19th century chairs that are set here and there. Without a shirt, the old upholstery is scratchy as fuck, but I let that go and close my eyes.

Okay, so Asheville is being overrun by Zs. That sucks. But why? Not why does it suck, but are the herds showing up now? In all the years since Z-Day there has never been this kind of activity.

We're up in the mountains, for fuck's sake. Zs don't naturally like going for a hike uphill. Unless...

Unless there is no more food where they have been so time to move along and look for the next exit with a Denny's.

Or...

Or someone is sending them this way.

Vance had thousands corralled in the drained Beaver Lake. He planned on using them as a weapon, whether for himself or for the fake POTUS Mondello, I don't know. That shit's still fuzzy and frankly I don't give a fuck since it's ancient history.

Or is it?

Think, Jace, fucking think!

Herds of Zs have made it up the mountains and are hell bent on plucking the delicious flesh from our bones. If we don't get the fuck out of here, the city will be a dead zone in days. If that long. If it is deliberate then why? Why clear out the living from Asheville? Why not send in armed assholes just to kill us?

Because we're armed too?

And maybe because...

"What's wrong with your shoulder, Long Pork?" Elsbeth asks as my eyes shoot open.

She's standing right in front of me, glaring.

"Oh, hey there, El," I say and scramble to try to get my t-shirt on, but the fucking one arm thing slows me down.

Elsbeth snatches the shirt from me and throws it to the floor.

"Are you going to tell me?" she asks.

"Tell you what?" I smile then look down at my shoulder. "Oh, that? It's nothing, just an old football injury flaring..."

She's right in my face, her nose touching mine, her eyes piercing mine, her hands on the arms of the chair, boxing me in.

"What's. Wrong. With. Your. Shoulder," she snarls. "It. Smells."

If you have paid attention to all my rambling then you know that a snarling Elsbeth is not a welcome thing in anyone's life.

A billion lies go through my head and I can tell Elsbeth sees every one of them behind my eyes. I say the wrong thing and she's going to kick my ass.

"Soldiers," I blurt.

This confuses her, which doesn't necessarily make things safer, but she does ease back an inch or two.

"What?" she asks. "What soldiers?"

I tell her what's going down.

"Are they our soldiers?" Elsbeth asks.

"I don't know," I say. "I hope so."

She looks at my shoulder then up at the windows. I hold my breath as I wait for her decision on a course of action. Will it be what's behind Door Number One and the kicking of Jace's ass? Or what's behind Door Number Two and the...

She throws my shirt in my face.

"Get that on," she says. "Come on. We're going to see if it's our soldiers."

"Sounds like a plan" I say as I stand up.

"But," she growls, a finger poking me in the chest. I notice this time she keeps her eyes averted from my wound. "But, we talk later. And you give me the truth."

There's no argument in that statement.

"Yeah, yeah," I nod, "of course."

***

"I said...turn that...fucking light...off," Platt groans. "You're...giving away..."

"Our position," Reaper finishes for him. "I know, but if I don't get this bleeding under control you won't make it to Whispering Pines."

Platt grinds his teeth as Reaper digs into the wound, hoping to find the bleed. He swears and curses under his breath as the light from his headlamp shows him nothing.

"It's down in there," Reaper says. "I don't know how far, but I can't find the bullet. Fuck!"

"Leave...me," Platt says.

"Fuck you," John replies as he crouches down by the raft as it rests on the rocky boat landing. "You keep saying that and we keep saying no. You're wasting our time, Master Sergeant."

"I order...you," Platt whispers.

Reaper shakes his head as he repacks Platt's wound. "You aren't in any shape to give orders. As current medical officer, I relieve you of duty. Sorry, Platt, your orders don't mean shit anymore."

"Fuck...you," Platt sighs.

"Shhh," John says. "Company."

Reaper turns the light off instantly and grabs his rifle. He wishes he had some night vision goggles, but that luxury is long gone. He has to rely on his ears to pierce the night.

The two men wait for several minutes, but don't hear anything. Yet, being Special Forces, they know better than to take anything for granted. Reaper can just make out John moving in the darkness as he crouch-walks his way up the boat landing and fully onto shore. He loses sight of the sniper completely and waits.

Platt moans in the raft and Reaper cringes at how loud the noise is. The Master Sergeant must have passed out or he wouldn't have made a sound. Even in excruciating pain, Platt knows to stay silent. Reaper sweeps the rifle left then right, his senses straining to pick something, anything, up.

There's a grunt, a shout, and the sharp bark of John's rifle. Then silence.

Reaper's finger that was resting along the trigger guard, now touches lightly on the trigger itself.

"Don't," a voice says from his right.

Reaper whirls about, ready to open fire, but he takes a fist to his jaw and goes sprawling. Hands grab him and he tries to fight them off, but a fist slams again and again into his face until he's too stunned to move.

"Fuck," he mutters as he's dragged up the landing and tossed next to an unconscious John.

In the dim light, Reaper can just make out about six figures circled around him. He doesn't see the outlines of weapons, so he thinks he may make it out alive. Although, if the blows to his head are any indication of what's possible, it won't take a bullet to knock his brains out, those fists will do the job easily.

"Who are you?" he asks, tensing for a kick to shut him up. That's usually been his experience.

"You first," a woman orders, "and no bullshit."

"No bullshit?" Reaper laughs. "You knock out my teammate and beat the fuck out of my face and call bullshit on *me*? Fuck you, bitch."

A couple of the figures giggle. Wait...giggle?

Then the kick comes.

"Fuck!" Reaper yells.

"Stop!" a man's voice calls out from the darkness. "Don't hurt them!"

Reaper knows that voice. Only one man sounds like that kind of grit.

"Stuart?" Reaper asks. "Stuart!"

Stuart hurries up to the group and shoves a couple of the women out of the way. He kneels by Reaper and looks him over.

"You okay, Reaper?" Stuart asks. "How bad are you hurt?"

"Busted lip and pretty sure I'll have a fucker of a black eye," Reaper says as Stuart helps him sit up. "But it's Platt that needs help."

"Platt?" Stuart asks glancing at John. "That looks like John, not Platt."

"Platt's in the raft," Reaper says. "He's been shot and bleeding out. We're trying to get to Whispering Pines, but I knew he wouldn't make it so we stopped here. Hey...what the hell are you doing here? This is the Biltmore, right?"

"Long fucking story," Stuart says. "Come on, let me help you up."

"You know them?" Cassie asks, getting in front of Stuart and Reaper.

"Yeah, they're friends," Stuart says. "I'm sure you've seen them before. They're part of the Special Ops Team that's been helping us."

"We're all that's left of the Special Ops Team," Reapers adds.

"They're the ones that went down to Atlanta," a woman says.

"Right," Cassie nods. She looks at the others. "Help get the wounded man up to the house. Get him into the surgery."

"The what?" Reaper asks. "The surgery? What the hell are you talking about?"

"Hey," a woman says as she slaps John's face. "Hey, wake up. Sorry I knocked you out."

John stirs and then starts to strike out, but his fists are easily knocked away.

"Hey!" the woman snaps and smacks John across the face. "I said I was sorry!"

The women all move as John scrambles backwards. "What the fuck?"

"Calm down," Cassie says, "your friends are here."

"Hey, John," Melissa says as she helps him to his feet.

"Reaper?" John asks.

"Right here, man," Reaper responds.

"Uh, okay," John says, "I'm confused."

"It sounds like your friend is dying," Cassie says as the women all walk down to the raft. "We'll try not to let that happen."

They pull the raft up further then split up and get on each side, lifting the raft like an oversized, rubber stretcher. Stuart and the rest move out of the way, as they start the long hike back to the house.

"Brittany?" Cassie says. "Take the soldiers and hurry up to the house. Show them where the surgery is so the medic can prep. And find Antoinette. Tell her she's going to be operating tonight."

"Sure," Brittany, the one that knocked John out, says as she taps Reaper and John on the shoulders then takes off running. "Follow me."

The men don't hesitate and take off, with Stuart on their heels, after the woman that is already several yards away.

"Need my help?" Melissa asks as she watches the women carry the raft.

"No," Cassie says. "Go with your friends."

"I think I'll stay with Platt," Melissa says.

"Don't trust us?" Cassie laughs.

"Don't trust anyone," Melissa says, "except my daddy and brothers."

***

"That ain't good," Pup whispers as they all stare at the herd of Zs that cover Merrimon Ave, blocking their way to Reynolds Mountain.

Explosions and gunfire can be heard further south in the city, but Lourdes ignores those sounds and focuses on the task at hand: getting the residents of Whispering Pines to safety. Which is a task made harder by a pissed off Stella Stanford.

"If it wasn't for my children I'd say fuck it to this plan," Stella says at Lourdes's side. "I vowed never to take charity from that bitch."

"She's not there," Lourdes says. "She is with your husband, last I heard."

"What?" Stella asks.

"She was picked up and they were heading to the Counsel meeting when everything went bad," Lourdes says. "They were going to help at the power plant."

"What? Where are they now? Do you know where Jace is?" Stella snaps, her voice a barely controlled whisper. Some moans from the herd make Lourdes give her a harsh look.

"I don't know anything," Lourdes whispers. "We lost track when communications went down. What I'm worried about is why my people aren't here. I sent them to evac the GPI. Must still be up at the main community digging in."

A massive explosion and resulting fireball makes everyone hit the ground. Except Lourdes. She stares at the fading light of the fire and calculates the distance to the explosion. And the direction.

"Shit," she says. "That's my assault Teams. Not good."

What is good is the sound attracts the attention of the herd and many of the Zs turn about and start shambling back south down Merrimon Ave the way they came. It isn't long before the mass has thinned out enough that Lourdes motions for her people to get ready. She tugs on Stella's arm and pulls her back to the Humvee, glancing at the caravan of miscellaneous vehicles that are lined up behind them along Woodfin Ave.

She turns to Pup and leans in close, keeping her voice low. "Spread word that we are making a break for it," she says. "No one starts their vehicle until I give the signal. Once the zeds hear our engines they'll swarm again. We have only a small window to get across Merrimon and up the road to the Reynolds Mountain encampment before they are on us. Got it?"

Pup nods and runs down the row of vehicles, passing on the information to each driver.

Lourdes looks at Stella. "Get in and get ready," she says then looks at her driver. "When I give the signal you don't stop 'til Brooklyn."

"A Beastie Boys reference?" Charlie says from the backseat. "I don't think that really applies here."

"Hey kid?" Lourdes says as she looks over her shoulder. "Nobody fucking asked you."

"Nobody didn't *not* fucking ask me," Charlie glares.

"I think you have that backwards," she replies.

"You fuck," Charlie snaps. "How's that for backwards?"

"Fair enough," Lourdes says, cutting Charlie some slack.

They all strap in and Lourdes holds her arm out the window. She watches the Zs moving then drops her hand. Every vehicle in the convoy starts up at once.

"Go!" Lourdes shouts.

The driver punches it and the Humvee shoots across Merrimon, wiping out Zs that stand in its way. Guts and black blood splatter up onto the windshield, but the driver doesn't care as the Humvee thumps and bumps over rotten corpses. He cranks the wheel and takes a hard left as they get across and race up the hill towards Reynolds Mountain Village, a group of misused buildings that were supposed to hold retail shops as well as residential condos.

Sales kinda went to shit when the dead started walking the Earth.

Lourdes looks back at the convoy and sees several vehicles following right behind. But she also sees that several are still on the far side of Merrimon and not moving.

"Fuck," she says, causing everyone else to turn and look.

"Why are they just sitting there?" Stella asks, watching as the Zs notice the stationary vehicles. "They need to move!"

"One of them must have broken down," the driver says, "it's blocking the others."

"Don't stop," Lourdes says.

"Wasn't planning on it," the driver frowns.

"But what about them?" Greta asks. "We can't leave them!"

111

"We're taking you up to the gates," Lourdes says. "Then we'll go back and help."

The driver barely uses the brakes as he rockets through the twists and turns that take them to the entrance of the Reynolds Mountain estate. When he gets there, he turns the Humvee in a wide arc so it's facing back down the hill. Lourdes hops out and starts waving for others to do the same.

"Everyone out except a driver and shooter!" Lourdes orders. "We're going back down to get the rest!"

The vehicles empty and the residents of Whispering Pines instantly rush forward towards Stella as she stands there, motioning them to her

"Stay safe," Lourdes says as she gets back into the Humvee and it speeds off.

"Did she seriously just say that?" Charlie asks. "That lady be loco, yo."

Terrified eyes look expectantly at Stella and she nods to them all.

"Stay close to each other and don't let anyone wander off," Stella says. "Hold tight as I get us inside."

"I thought Lourdes said there would be PCs here with the Grove Park people," Greta says. "They were supposed to dig in and be ready for the Zs." She looks around. "I don't see anything."

"That's because it's too dark to see," Charlie says.

"You know what I mean," Greta snaps.

"Stop," Stella orders and the kids go quiet. She walks up to the gates and bangs her palm against them. "Hello?"

"Sorry, ma'am," a man says from above, "but I can't let you in."

"It's me," Stella says. "Stella Stanford. We had to evacuate Whispering Pines. There's a huge herd of Zs taking over the city. Please let us in now."

"I know who you are, Ms. Stanford, but I'm under strict orders not to let anyone in," the man replies before swallowing hard and continuing. "I'm especially not to let anyone from Whispering Pines in. Particularly anyone named Stanford."

"That fucking cunt," Stella mumbles then takes a deep breath. "I'm sure Brenda gave that order, I have *zero* doubt about that, but things have changed. This isn't about petty squabbles. This is about people living or dying. Please, you have to let us in."

"Ma'am, I'm sorry, but if I do that then they'll kick me and my whole family outside the wire," the man says. "We won't survive out there."

"Let us the fuck in, asshole!" someone shouts.

"Open the gates!" another voice rings out.

"There are children!" a woman screams.

"Please! My wife is hurt!"

"Help us!"

"Please!"

"Please!"

"PLEASE!"

The group is lit up by floodlights from the top of the gates and everyone shields their eyes from the glare.

"BACK OFF!" a voice booms. "If you don't leave we will open fire! We do not allow bums into Reynolds Mountain!"

"What did you call us?" Stella replies. "Are you joking? You'll open fire. Who is that?"

"I'm the deputy head of security while Mindy Starling is away," the voice says. "That's all you need to know, Ms. Stanford. I have been authorized by our mayor to kill any threats to the security of this community."

"Mayor? Mayor! Is that what that Jabba the Hut wannabe cunt is calling herself?"

"Mom," Charlie cautions, but Stella ignores him.

"Listen deputy in charge of sucking my dick, open these fucking gates! Your precious *mayor* is a psychopathic bitch that's done nothing but harm since..."

A shot rings out and Stella screams as a spark kicks up in the pavement in front of her.

The gunfire instantly panics the crowd and they rush the gates. Stella grabs Greta and Charlie to her as they are shoved forward.

Then the shots start raining down.

Stella has no idea how many are up there, but enough to steadily keep firing as the refugees are helplessly slaughtered in front of the gates. She pulls her children with her and turns towards the woods that line the lane leading to the community. She cries out in pain as a bullet singes the back of her neck, but it doesn't slow her. Her only thoughts are on getting her children to safety.

"Get down!" Stella shouts as she shoves Greta and Charlie ahead of her into the darkness of the young pines. "Get behind the trees and stay down!"

"Mom!" Greta yells. "Where are you going?"

"I'm going to get Lourdes!" Stella shouts as she turns and rushes down the road. "Stay down!"

Fighting every instinct in her body, Stella races down the winding road back towards Merrimon. The mother in her is screaming for her to go back, grab her children, and hunker down. But the leader inside her slaps the mother aside and screams that there are other people's children being murdered and she has to stop it.

If it was just fighting Zs she could have rallied the refugees together; she's good at that. But fighting other people? Especially when some of those people used to be her neighbors? Well, she needs Lourdes for that job.

But that's not in the plan.

Something slams into Stella's side, sending her tumbling off the road and into the thorny underbrush. A snarl and the stench tell her it's a Z that's got her pinned against the trunk of a pine tree. Stella hammers at the thing's face. It snaps at her, but she is able to get her hand up under its chin and push. She keeps pushing and pushing until she hears the snap of the Z's neck.

She kicks out from under the thing and scrambles to her feet. The road is just in front of her, but so is a group of Zs. They must have followed up after the convoy. Stella counts eight, nine, ten, eleven of them and does some quick estimates. She realizes that staying in the woods is safer.

Barely able to make out roots and small bushes, Stella scrambles down the hillside towards Merrimon Ave, praying the whole way she doesn't fall and snap her neck. And praying that Lourdes and the others aren't overwhelmed.

**

The snap of a branch makes Charlie and Greta turn their attention from the massacre of their neighbors to the woods behind them.

"What's that?" Charlie whispers.

"A raccoon?" Greta asks.

But that guess is quickly proven wrong as a Z stumbles from behind a tree and lunges at the two teenagers. Greta screams as the thing falls on top of her. Its jaws snap at her face and she barely keeps it away by shoving her forearm up against its throat. The only problem is that the flesh around the throat is mushy and rotten, meaning that Greta can't get enough leverage and the Z's jaws just get closer and closer.

Until its head goes flying off.

"Holy shit," Greta says as she looks up at her brother standing over her with a hunk of deadwood in his hand. "Thanks."

Charlie helps her up then looks up the hill. "Come on."

"Where are we going?" Greta asks.

"The gate doesn't wrap around the whole mountain," Charlie says. "There has to be another way in."

"I heard they razor wired everything," Greta says. "Like several layers."

"Yeah, I heard that too," Charlie says as they make their way in the dark blindly towards the fence line. "But that's to keep Zs out. We aren't Zs. Maybe we can squeeze through or climb over."

They go a few more yards, angling off to the left so they can put some distance between them and the continuing gunfire. It's a treacherous hike, and both of them slip and nearly fall back down the hillside, but they finally get to the first string of razor wire.

And stare at what's before them, neither hiding the fact they want to cry.

"What the fuck?" Charlie says.

"Zs aren't that tall," Greta says as she looks at the razor wire.

Lines of shiny metal are nailed into the pine trees starting at about six inches off the ground and continuing every six inches up the trunk.

"It goes up like twelve feet," Charlie says as he cranes his neck to look at the top most row. "Why?"

"Because it's not meant to just keep Zs out," Greta says. "These assholes want to keep people out too."

"What do we do now?" Charlie asks.

The teens can see beyond the first row of razor wire is a second row and then a third, possibly a fourth. Even if they could figure out how to get through the wire that is directly in front of them, they'd have even more to deal with. Greta walks forward and pushes down on the wire, keeping her hands away from the sharp parts.

"It's solid," Greta says, close to tears. "No give at all."

"Fuck," Charlie says, "then we stay here and wait?"

"I guess…" Greta trails off.

"What?" Charlie whispers.

"Shhh," Greta says.

Charlie listens hard and realizes the gunfire has stopped.

"Does that mean they're all dead?" Charlie asks.

"Shhh," Greta says again.

Then Charlie hears it. Moans. A lot of them. He grips the deadwood he still holds in his hand, his back to the razor wire fence.

"At least they can't get us from behind," he says.

Greta gets on her hands and knees and feels around until she finds what she needs. Slapping her own hunk of deadwood against her palm to test its weight, she looks over at her brother.

"Love you," she says.

"Love you, too," Charlie replies.

Then they see the first shapes coming towards them.

* * *

Stella nearly falls over the edge of the rock wall that lines Merrimon Ave at the base of Reynolds Mountain Village. Her arms pinwheel and she grabs onto a rhododendron to keep from falling into the street. Dirt and leaves kick out from under her shoes and rain down on the Zs below her. Some look up and start to hiss, their arms reaching for the meal that was delivered above them.

"Fuck," Stella mutters, seeing that her way is blocked.

She knows the gunfire from above has stopped which scares the shit out of her, but the gunfire in front of her is still going. She looks down the street and can see a barricade of vehicles at the entrance to Reynolds Mountain Village and the bright flashes from rifles. Not known for her balancing skills, Stella has to use all of her concentration to keep from falling as she tightrope walks the edge of the wall towards the fighting.

"Fuck!" Lourdes shouts as she turns her rifle on Stella. "I almost shot you!"

"They're killing them!" Stella yells over the gunfire as Lourdes helps her down behind the Humvee and other vehicles that keep the mass of Zs from taking them all.

"Good!" Lourdes shouts. "We were hoping you could take care of the Zs! Sorry they followed us up when…"

"No! NO!" Stella screams. "They're killing *us*! The motherfuckers are shooting *us*!"

Lourdes doesn't say anything, as her mind whirls a mile a minute, trying to piece together what Stella has just said.

"Wait…what?" she asks finally. "Who's killing who?"

"The fucking Reynolds people!" Stella yells. "They're slaughtering us! They refused to let us in and when some of the residents rushed the gates they just opened fire!"

Lourdes puts her hand to her mouth. "Jesus Christ…"

"Greta and Charlie are still up there!" Stella yells. "We have to help them! We have to help everyone!"

"I thought the gunfire was the guards shooting the Zs," Lourdes says, looking up the road. "I never thought…my God…" She takes a deep breath and shakes it off like a professional. "We'll need backup, but we can't take everyone."

She looks down the line at the people firing at the Zs that are trying to get up over the vehicles.

"Grab the Fitzpatricks!" she yells at Stella. "I'll go ahead and clear the way!"

"What about your people? They'll fight better!" Stella cries.

"I need them to stay down here and hold the line," Lourdes yells. "Get the Fitzpatricks!"

Lourdes takes off up the hill as Stella runs to the huge farm boys that are standing behind a pickup truck. Buzz and Porky are firing into the herd of Zs while Pup reloads rifles, handing them to his brothers the second theirs shoot empty.

"Boys!" Stella shouts at the men that are anything but. Each one towers over her. "Help!"

Buzz spins about and she fills him in. Even in the darkness of the night, Stella can see his face grow redder and redder with rage. The men quickly grab up every bit of ammunition they can shove in their pockets and race up the hill. Stella is right behind them, but her short legs can't keep up with the stronger, faster men.

Soon she's alone on the road, her lungs burning and the muscles in her legs ready to cramp up. But she pushes past that because all she can think about are her babies.

"Please let them be safe," Stella prays, "please."

***

Greta doesn't need light to know the color of the gunk that splatters across her face as she crushes the skull of a Z that lunges for her. It's black. It's always black. She ducks to her left and lets another attacking Z rush past her. It quickly gets tangled in the razor wire to hers and her brother's backs and starts to shred itself as it struggles to get loose.

"Down!" Charlie shouts as he swings towards Greta.

She ducks as Charlie's hunk of deadwood whooshes over her head and slams into the face of a Z that had gotten caught earlier. The force of the blow, coupled with the sharpness of the razor wire and the softness of the creature's neck, results in a very messy decapitation. Charlie kicks the snapping head down the hill at the other Zs as they come at the siblings.

"Use the fence!" Charlie shouts.

"I know!" Greta replies as she sweeps the legs out from under a Z and watches it tumble into others.

"Get them caught in the wire!" Charlie yells, ripping the jaw off a Z with an uppercut blow.

"I know!" Greta replies again, this time as she brings her deadwood flat against the chest of a Z, caving in its softened ribcage. It slows it down enough for Greta to use her momentum and spin completely around, increasing the force of her hit as she nails the Z in the temple. Its entire head crumples under the force and rotting brains spill out from the shattered skull.

"If we trap enough we can use the razors against them!" Charlie shouts.

"I KNOW!" Greta screams. "SHUT UP!"

Charlie uses his elbow to shove a Z to the side as he kicks another in the knee, shattering the thing's leg. It crumples and Charlie brings his wood down hard on the Z's skull, silencing it forever. The limp body rolls down the hill towards the other stilled corpses.

The Z that Charlie had knocked aside reaches for him, but he ducks under the arms and rams it in the chest with his shoulder, driving it up against the wire fence. The monster struggles, struggles, then breaks free as most of the putrid flesh from its back tears off in drippy strips. But Charlie uses its forward momentum, and good old gravity, against it and sticks out his leg, easily tripping the Z.

It falls face first into the dirt and Charlie brings his wood down on the back of its skull. The first blow just shoves the Z's face into the soft earth, but the second blow splits bone and the thing stops moving.

Charlie is barely able to get the hunk of deadwood up in time to fend off another attacking Z. It grips his shirt and tries to pull him forward, but he jams it in the chest with the end of the deadwood and shoves it away. The sudden loosening of the Z's grip sends Charlie stumbling backwards and he screams as his arms are sliced by the razor wire behind him.

The fresh blood sends the remaining Zs into a frenzy and their usual shambling attacks turn quickly into a full on rush. Greta steps forward, not wanting to have a repeat of what happened to Charlie happen to her, and kicks out with her right leg, nailing the first Z in the gut. Soft, fetid intestines spill out around her foot as the Z's belly splits open. She swallows the gorge that rises in her throat and concentrates on keeping her traction as she almost loses her balance when her gore slicked foot comes back down.

The Z snarls at her and lunges, but gets tangled in its own guts as they spill from its midsection and slide around its legs. Greta bashes the thing's head in before it can get free of its bowels.

Greta's gorge wins this time, she turns her head, and projectile pukes against a small pine tree.

"Sorry," she says to the pine as she wipes her mouth with the back of her hand.

"They keep coming!" Charlie yells.

"I know!" Greta replies.

"Oh, don't start that again!" Charlie laughs. It's a strained, almost maniacal laugh, but it must be contagious because Greta joins in with him.

The Zs don't know that the sounds they hear are two teenagers laughing at the insanity of everything; they just know food is in front of them. And they lunge, their ever present hunger pushing them towards death, whether the teenagers' or theirs.

***

"Oh, sweet God," Lourdes says as she reaches the scene of the massacre in front of the gates. "What have you done?"

"Get back, woman!" a man shouts. "We know who you are! You better listen or you go down like your frei..."

Lourdes has her rifle up and firing before he can finish. She barely aims, just shoots at the head shaped shadows that line the top of the gates. Screams and cries of pain tell her she hits her marks. The fact that there's no return fire tells her she hit every mark. Her last few shots kill the spotlights that glare down at her.

Covered in Z gore, the Fitzpatricks come rushing up behind her.

"Damn," Buzz says. "Didn't really need us, did ya?"

"We still need to get inside those gates," Lourdes says. "And then deal with the fuckers behind them."

"I can do it," Porky says as he eyes the logs that make up the structure before them. "I like climbing."

"He does," Pup nods. "My brother can climb a tree faster than a possum with a hound on its butt."

Stella, gasping for air, stumbles up to Lourdes, Buzz and Pup, as Porky runs to the gate and begins his ascent. He's halfway up when a face peers over the side. Lourdes puts a bullet right between the face's eyes.

"Jesus," Buzz says. "Maybe they weren't gonna hurt him."

"You really want to take that chance?" she asks, sweeping her arm about at the corpses that litter the road.

The corpses...

"Ah, shit," Pup says then looks at Buzz. "Pardon my language."

"Daddy's dead, Pup," Buzz says.

"But he still wouldn't like me cussin'," Pup says.

Buzz gives his brother a sad smile and nods.

A couple of the corpses start to wiggle and shake.

"They're coming back," Stella says. "Oh, God, they're coming back."

Lourdes pulls her baton as Buzz and Pup turn their rifles around, butts down.

By the time the gates slowly creak open, the refugees that tried to reanimate are silenced for good. Buzz, Lourdes, Pup, and Stella stand there with silent tears streaming down their faces.

Then a high pitched scream echoes from the pines to their left.

"GRETA!" Stella shouts and runs towards the sound.

"Stella! Wait!" Lourdes yells, but it does no good, the woman is gone into the darkness of the woods. "Shit!"

More screams fill the air.

"I got this," Buzz says. "Take my brothers inside there and kick some ass! I'll make sure the Stanfords are okay!"

***

Branches whip at her face, but Stella doesn't care. Her babies are in trouble, her little girl is screaming! With each piercing shriek, something dies inside Stella until she feels like a hollow shell of the woman that just seconds ago rushed into the woods without a second thought.

"GRETA!" Stella screams, knowing her voice will attract more Zs, but not giving two flying fucks of a shit. "GRETA!"

Stella rounds a turn in the hillside and slides to a halt, her mouth open at the scene before her. She tries to walk forward, but her legs won't move; they are frozen to the spot. Without warning, her knees buckle and she falls onto them, her hands out in front of herself so she doesn't completely face plant.

"Mrs. Stanford!" Pup yells behind her.

"Stella!" Buzz shouts.

The two men nearly run over her as they come around the turn. The rifle in Pup's hand clatters to the dirt as he stares at the carnage that covers the area.

"What the holy hell?" Buzz whispers.

The two Stanford teenagers are busy slamming their wooden weapons down over and over and over.

"Greta?" Stella says. "Charlie?"

Charlie stops and gives his mom a maniacal smile. He straightens up and points his weapon.

"Greta, stop," he says. "Mom's here."

Greta freezes, her hunk of deadwood raised over her head, and looks to where Charlie points. At their feet is what once was a Z, but is now a demolished pile of bone and pulpy flesh. Some of that flesh drips off the deadwood and onto Greta's face and she casually wipes it away.

"Mom!" Greta shouts as she runs forward and dives at her mother, wrapping her arms about Stella in a chest crushing embrace.

"Hey, Mom," Charlie says as he walks over to them. "Greta lost it there for a minute." He shrugs. "I may have gone with her a bit."

"Did you two…?" Buzz asks then stops and shakes his head.

"Kill them all?" Pup finishes for his brother.

Charlie looks over his shoulder at the Z corpses that litter the ground and hang from the fence. He shrugs.

"Yeah," he says, "I guess we did."

"You guess you did?" Stella cries. "You guess you did? My, God, I thought you two were dead when I heard Greta scream! Get over here!"

Charlie kneels and lets his mother pull him against her and his sister. Stella can't hold it together and begins to sob uncontrollably.

"My babies," she whispers, "my sweet, sweet babies."

"Uh, Buzz?" Pup whispers. "We need to get back and help Ms. Torres."

"Give it a minute," Buzz says. "We are needed here right now. I sure ain't one to hurry a mama bear when she's huggin' her cubs."

Pup nods and smiles at the Stanfords then reaches down and picks up his rifle. He puts it to his shoulder and watches the area, his eyes looking deep into the shadows, keeping the hugging and crying family safe from any more harm.

For the moment.

CHAPTER SIX

"That's quite a story," I say, handing John a bottle of water as we all sit on the long porch of the Biltmore House. "All of the Zs came from Atlanta?"

"Not all," John replies. "Most of them were probably picked up along the way in Athens then in Greenville/Spartanburg. The Consortium has been hoarding them for years."

"Hoarding hordes," I say, shaking my head. "I guess after what Mondello said, I shouldn't be surprised."

"What about other groups then?" Stuart asks, leaning forward in his chair. "Lourdes has mentioned that there are quite a few more enclaves like Atlanta across the country."

"I don't know," John shrugs, "we didn't hear much about them. They are out there, but I don't think there's any unity between them. More like the city/states of Italy."

"The what?" Melissa asks.

"The city/states," I reply for John. Because I can't help being the know it all. And my shoulder fucking hurts so I need to talk, to do anything to get my mind off it. "Italy used to be made up of city/states that each had their own king. Florence, Naples, Venice, Rome, etc. Each had its strengths and weaknesses, but all had armies. They worked together when it came to foreign countries like France invading or Spain. Unless it was more advantageous to work with the invaders. Naples was notorious for that. Working with the French, working against the French, working with the French. Blah blah blah."

"Great," Stuart nods, "that info doesn't help us at all."

"But it gives us perspective," I counter. "As we all know, history repeats itself. We learn from the past and we'll be able to predict the future."

"So what are we in this future?" Melissa asks. "France? Pardon me, but I don't want to be French."

"Don't you mean *pardonne moi*?" I grin.

"Fuck off, Stanford," Melissa smirks.

"So who do we work with then?" Stuart asks, looking at John.

"I don't know," he replies. "I hear there's Boulder, Kansas City, Salt Lake, Portland, and probably others."

"What about New York or LA?" Melissa asks. "They aren't players?"

"They don't exist," John says. "That much we know for sure. The populations were too big. The Zs wiped everything out and there's no way anyone can get in and secure those places. Not that they'd want to. I heard a rumor that LA was torched. They burned it to the ground."

"Nuclear?" Stuart asks.

"Don't think so," John answers. "As far as I know no one has gone nuclear. Not yet."

"And that's what that is?" Melissa asks, nodding towards the pack far down the porch, away from all of them. "A nuke?"

"No, no," John says. "It's spent uranium wrapped in a very large amount of C4. A dirty bomb."

"But not the only one," Stuart says.

"Probably not," John agrees.

"Having that makes me think Atlanta wasn't going to go take muffins to the other cities," Stuart says.

"Why?" Melissa asks. "Why bother?"

"Resources," I say, "and control. The Consortium is not made up of Boy Scouts. It's not a non-profit organization. They had Mondello in their pocket and he was the, and I use the term lightly, President of the United States."

"But why not send Zs into the cities like they are doing to us?" Melissa asks.

"Because that's a lot of distance," John says. "And the cities are prepared for herds of Zs. What they aren't prepared for is radiation and their people dying brutal deaths from that."

"Salt the earth," I say.

"Jesus," Stuart says.

"Holy shit," Melissa nods, getting it. "They blow one of these up and the city is dead in what, months?"

"Yeah, about close to that," John says.

"Then the place is contaminated and now new folk can't move in and rebuild," Melissa says. "It's like poisoning an ant hill or wasps nest."

"Exactly," I say.

"Huh," Elsbeth grunts as she sits on the porch rail. She'd been so quiet I forgot about her. "Why do we have one?"

"What?" John asks.

"Why do we have a bomb?" Elsbeth asks again. "Why take it? What do we need it for?"

"In case," John says and frowns. "I voted against, so did Reaper. But Platt…"

"Platt's an old soldier," Stuart says, "not as old as me, but old enough to know a deterrent when he saw one."

"Deter what?" Elsbeth says. "They have already won."

"I don't know if they've won or…," John begins but stops as several loud explosions echo across the estate.

We all get up and look towards the north, but the house blocks our view. We scramble inside and race through the house to the other side. Many of the sisters join us as we run upstairs to a row of north facing windows.

Asheville is on fire. We can see huge flames licking the darkness of early morning sky. Another explosion goes off then another. We're all thinking it, but I'm the one that voices it. Since I can't keep my mouth shut.

"We can't rebuild this," I say, "Asheville is lost." A trillion thoughts flood through my mind, but the main one is. "Whispering Pines."

"I can't tell where the fire is exactly," John says. "It may not be that close."

"Doesn't matter," I say. "It's not like the fire department is going to put out those blazes. It'll spread and wipe everything out that can burn. And considering the dry summer we've had, that means it'll burn all the way to the river."

"My lord," Melissa says, "what do we do?"

"That is something to talk about," Cassie says as she joins us. Reaper is right behind.

"Platt?" John asks.

"He'll make it," Reaper nods, "thanks to Antoinette. She's still in there, watching his vitals. I told her I'd do it, but she is pretty focused. Like she's been waiting for this."

"She has," Cassie says. "We all have our specialties. Antoinette studied surgery. Unfortunately for her, none of us has had more than a few scrapes that needed stitches. I've never seen her so happy."

"Yep," I nod, "you are Elsbeth's sisters alright."

"What does that mean?" Elsbeth scowls.

"Just that y'all have a different definition of 'happy' and 'unfortunately'," I smile, hoping she doesn't punch me.

"True," Elsbeth nods.

Far off are the sounds of rifles. They stop then start again then stop. We all stand by the window and face the burning glow of Asheville.

"I have to assume that's Lourdes and her PCs," Stuart says. "Hopefully, they are the buffer between the Zs and Whispering Pines."

"Wish we had communications," John says, "that would make things easier."

"You're soldiers," one of the sisters (Stacy? Tracy?) says, "use your radios."

"Jammed," John replies, "not a single signal."

"Hmmmm," Cassie says and looks at the other women. "We knew the Wi-Fi went down..."

"What is it?" Elsbeth asks. "You know something. Tell us. Now."

"*Us*, sister?" Cassie smiles. "What *us* would that be?"

Elsbeth just glares. Cassie holds up her hands in apology.

"My bad. I was playing," Cassie says. "Audrey reported men setting up equipment on top of the BB&T building. Right in the center of town."

"The jammer," John smiled, "if we can take that down then we can coordinate everyone again."

"The Consortium will be listening, I'm sure," Cassie says.

"Let them," I smile, "they can hear what's coming for them."

"I'll go," Stuart says.

"I'm in," John nods.

"I will go too and kill the jammer with my bare hands," Elsbeth says. "I liked my Wi-Fi."

"Some of us will go as well," Cassie says. "Let me speak to my sisters. The rest will accompany you to Whispering Pines."

"Wait...what?" Melissa asks. "How? The roads are full of Zs. I know you ladies are badass and all, but not take-out-a-million-Zs badass. No offense, meant. I'm all for strong women."

"We don't need roads," I say, "we have the French Broad."

"That was our plan," Reaper says, "before Platt got so bad. We were going to float into Riverside Park down across the highway from Whispering Pines. We still can."

"If the Zs haven't over taken it," Stuart says then sees the look on my face. "Sorry, Jace."

"No, no, it's cool," I nod. "I'm sure Stella has it all under control."

God, I hope so...

***

"Close the gates now!" Stella screams as the last Humvee races through with a herd of Zs on its ass.

The massive gates slowly swing shut, just before the wave of undead slam into them. The sounds of a thousand decaying hands roll up over the gates and bounce around the Reynolds Mountain community. The residents stand around, most of them stricken with fear, but some glaring daggers at Lourdes and her PCs.

"You have no right to be here!" a man snaps. "Brenda Kelly brought us here to get away from your chaos!"

"Shut the fuck up," Stella shouts. "Brenda Kelly is a self-centered bitch. And not here right now."

"Hey, tone it down, Ms. Stanford," Buzz says, "they're just scared."

"They murdered our friends! Our family!" Stella yells. "They should be scared! Scared of what I'm going to fucking do to them!"

"They didn't kill everyone," Lourdes says, looking towards the group of Whispering Pines residents that had hurried back to the gates once they realized they weren't going to be shot. Many had ducked into the woods to get away from the massacre, but were forced back when the Zs swarmed through the pines. "Let's be grateful some of us are still breathing."

Stella begins to respond, but Lourdes's words hit home. She looks over at her children and nods. The two teenagers are busy helping those that need it, regardless of where they are from.

"Fine," Stella says as she looks at the Reynolds people. "How far does the razor wire stretch? There's no way you had enough to encircle the whole community. We didn't even have enough for full repairs at Whispering Pines. We had to improvise...with..." Stella's newfound acceptance dissolves away and the rage returns. "You *fuckers*."

Lourdes realizes the conclusion Stella has come to and she steps between the woman and the Reynolds residents.

"Doesn't matter now," she says, giving Stella a hard look.

"They fucking stole our razor wire!" Stella says. "What else did you steal, huh? What else is there in this neighborhood that rightfully belongs to Whispering Pines?"

"We took what we needed," the man snaps. "You refused to share with us! We had to do what we had to do to keep our people safe!"

"Put them outside the gates!" Stella roars. "Fuck them! FUCK THEM ALL!"

"Mom, stop," Charlie says, "you sound like Brenda."

It's like a slap to the face with a fifty pound bag of cement. Stella actually staggers a step back, her eyes wide, as she looks at her son.

"He's right, Mom," Greta says, "you're scaring me." She looks at the people standing around, flinching at the sounds of the Zs separated from them by only a few feet of wood and metal. "You're scaring everyone."

Stella's legs go weak, but Buzz wraps his arm around her shoulders and keeps her upright.

"We need to stop and think," Buzz says. "Take some deep breaths and all work together. My daddy didn't build the Farm by blaming folks for what they did, but by accepting the changes they were willing to make."

"Amen," Pup and Porky say together.

"Good," Lourdes says. "We move past all the bickering and bullshit and start working on a plan to get us out of here."

"Out? Why?" a woman asks. "This is the safest place to be."

"Not anymore," Lourdes says. She does a quick head count. "I only have ten of my people and our ammunition is dangerously low. You all killed most of the Whispering Pines folks." She holds up her hands. "We aren't going into that again, so everyone keep their mouths shut. I mean *everyone*."

"What Ms. Torres is getting' at," Buzz says. "is we ain't got the resources to stay here. The Zs are gonna surround us completely and then it's only a matter of time before they get in. Or we starve."

"They'll get in first," Lourdes says. "Even with twelve foot high razor wire fencing, eventually it'll come down or enough zeds will pile on and be able to climb over each other. We need to work out how to leave."

"How many of us are there?" Stella asks, pulling herself together. "We need a head count. We need to know how many are wounded. We need to know who can run and who can't. We need to know how many vehicles you have in here."

"None," the man replies, "Brenda said there was no need for them. We had everything we needed here."

"Classic," Lourdes says, shaking her head. "Control movement. That woman is a piece of work."

"So no vehicles at all?" Stella asks.

The Reynolds people all shift about, but none say anything.

"Come on," Stella sighs, utterly exhausted. "I have teenagers. I know when people are hiding something."

"Hey!" Greta and Charlie say.

"Uh, well," the man frowns. "There may be one other thing we liberated from Whispering Pines. We expected you to come looking for it, but when you never did..."

"What? What is it?" Stella asks.

"We can show you," the man says, "follow me."

He turns and leads Buzz, Stella, Lourdes, and a few others up the road. They take a few turns, passing by completed and semi-completed houses, until they reach a house that is quite nearly a mansion.

"It's in the backyard," the man says, "only place we could hide it."

They all walk around the mini-mansion and stop.

"Son of a bitch," Stella says.

"That's where that went," Buzz frowns.

"I always thought you took it," Stella says to Lourdes. "For help with the power plant or the water system."

"I never touched it," Lourdes says. "My guess was Critter took off with it."

They all stare at the huge dump truck. A truck that had been only a mile away from Whispering Pines.

"Wait?" Buzz says when his uncle is mentioned. "Where *is* Critter?"

***

Dr. McCormick's lungs burn with exertion, but she doesn't dare stop. Once the Reynolds Mountain killers opened fire, she ran full speed into the woods. She ran and kept on running. At least until she hit a tree root and took a tumble halfway down the mountain. That trip ended with a hard hit to the head against one of the few oaks mingled in with the pine trees.

When she woke up, she saw shapes moving towards her. She didn't need to be told what they were. With her head bleeding and her body aching, she forced herself to get up and keep running. When she made it down the mountain, she found she was miles from the Reynolds estate entrance. But not alone.

So she runs and keeps running, using only adrenaline and willpower to keep her legs moving. The cramps that attack her muscles are excruciating and she knows it's only a matter of minutes before her body gives out. She is a doctor and understands the power of the mind, but a person can only push themselves so far before the body refuses to comply.

With the sounds of hungry Zs behind her, she acknowledges that her time is limited. Slowly, like a mantra, she begins listing everything she is grateful for or that she used to love before Z-Day. She has no intention of dying with her last thoughts being ones of fear or anger.

"Long baths," she starts, "with glasses of wine. Pumpkin pie with whipped cream. Sandra Bullock movies. A good pair of boots. Fitted bras. Funnel cakes. John Irving novels. Celebrity Apprentice. Hand sanitizer." Her list goes on and on, her voice growing weaker as her lungs start to hitch and give out.

"Fresh strawberries. Watermelon. The smell of cut grass. That pair of jeans I found at Goodwill when…" She stops talking to herself and listens hard. She hears the sounds of the Zs in pursuit, but there's also something else. "An engine…?"

She's running down the middle of Weaverville Highway with the burnt out husks of mini-strip malls to her left and right. Up ahead she sees what used to be Jimmy's Automotive and she swears she hears an engine. With the last bit of energy she can muster, she drives her legs forward towards the sound.

Stumbling over the broken pavement of the weed choked parking lot, Dr. McCormick falls to her knees. Before her is a closed garage bay door, behind her are a couple thousand Zs. She reaches out and is about to bang on the door when it lifts and starts rolling up into the ceiling. Instantly she's blinded by lights.

"What the holy hell?" a grizzled voice shouts. "Doc? That you? How the hell did…? Ah, shit. Get in, woman! Get up off your damn knees and get the fuck inside!"

Confused by it all, Dr. McCormick turns her head as someone grabs her and yanks her to her feet. "Wha…? Who…?"

"Get your ass in," the voice orders. "Looks like you brought company. And here I thought I had a good lead. But you shot that all to shit."

A seatbelt is suddenly strapped across her and Dr. McCormick jumps, as a door is slammed shut. She slowly shakes her head and looks about. She's in a car. No, no, that's not right.

She's in a Jeep.

And hopping into the driver's seat is someone she knows.

"Critter?" she croaks.

"Alive and kickin'," he grins at her as he puts the Jeep in gear and focuses on the swarm of Zs heading for the garage. "May wanna hang on tight, doc. And cover yer ears."

"Cover my-! AAAAAAAAHHHH!"

Her screams are drowned out as the roar of large caliber gunfire fills the garage. The Zs outside the bay door jump and shudder as they are torn apart. Critter lets out a barely heard whoop as he slams the gas pedal down and the Jeep rockets from the garage, bumping over undead corpses shredded by the two .50 caliber mini-guns bolted to the front of the Jeep.

Pulling his thumb from the trigger mounted on the gearshift, Critter focuses on steering past the Zs that still stand. He turns the Jeep in wide arcs, zooming back and forth as the Zs lunge for the vehicle. Instead of being able to grab onto the sides of the Jeep, they are sliced in half by huge blades welded to the doors and fenders.

"Woohoo!" Critter cries out, obviously enjoying himself. "Come on, ya bastards! Try and get me!"

The Zs do try, but they fail. All they get for their troubles are bellies ripped apart by 1 ¼ inch steel. While being mocked by an unrepentant highwayman.

Critter can see that the herd isn't going to thin out anytime soon, so he points the Jeep towards the highway and roars out of the parking lot, leaving the undead far behind him.

"Gonna head north for a bit, doc," Critter says. "We'll cut down to the river on Aiken Rd, up by Stoney Knob. Don't want to go too much further than that. Weaverville weren't never fully cleared out. We'll end up the meat in a Z herd sandwich."

"Critter?" Dr. McCormick asks. "How?"

"Now that's a pretty generic question, doc," Critter says. "I could answer that in a whole lotta ways. What you want answered first?"

Dr. McCormick slaps the dashboard of the Jeep.

"Oh, this thing?" he smiles. "I liberated it from the Grove Park. I believe it belonged to that Foster lady. That's what Long Pork done said. It were just sitting there collecting dust. A little too specialized for that Torres woman's taste, I guess. Or she just didn't want nothin' to do with it. Probably a little of both."

He glances over at Dr. McCormick. "It's a beauty, ain't it? Already had the guns, blades, and everything. I was planning on taking it back to my holler for safe keeping, but I only got it so far before it snapped a belt. Pushed the damn thing to Jimmy's myself a few weeks ago. Left it there, thinkin' to fix the belt at some point." He gives a little snort. "Turns out that point was tonight."

"But you were with us," Dr. McCormack rasps.

"Nah, I lit out on my own as soon as we hit Merrimon," Critter says. "I had no intention of getting trapped up on Reynolds Mountain. I just wanted to make sure Long Pork's family got there. I like them Stanfords. That Stella is a firecracker."

"Then you left?"

"Obviously," Critter snorts. "You hit your head or somethin'?"

"Yes," Dr. McCormick says. "But that's not why I asked. That means you didn't see what happened."

Critter's shit eating grin falters as he glances sideways at the doctor.

"What you talkin' 'bout? What happened?"

"They killed them," Dr. McCormick says, her voice almost lost in a sob. "The Reynolds Mountain people. They shot everyone. They're all dead."

Critter's eyes narrow and he takes a deep breath.

"Well, ain't that a shame," he says. "I ain't no saint, but even I have limits. That ain't right, killing folk like that."

He slams his hand on the dashboard making Dr. McCormick jump. By the glow of dashboard instruments, she can see the look of rage on Critter's face.

"Gonna have to be somethin' done," Critter snarls. "My brother was one to turn the other cheek." He glances over at Dr. McCormick with murder in his eyes. "But that's not my way. No, ma'am, people gonna die for that."

***

"You're going to die," Platt whispers as he listens to John and Stuart explain their plan. "You know that, right?"

"Yes, sir," John says, "it's certainly possible."

"More than possible," Platt says. "Now that we know the city has been overrun."

"It's the only way," I interrupt. "Unless we can reestablish communications we won't know where everyone is. We got stupid and spread out. There's the Grove Park and Reynolds Mountain as well as Whispering Pines."

"Plus the Farm," Melissa says. "The herds could be all the way out there by now."

"We have to be able to talk to everyone," I insist. "Otherwise we could end up going to save people that are already dead."

That sinks in. Hard. Already dead.

Stella, Charlie, Greta...

I shake the thought off.

Platt is watching me, knowing what is going through my head.

"Go over the plan again," he says.

"You need to rest," Antoinette says, glaring at us as we crowd around Platt's bed in the infirmary.

"I'll rest when I'm dead," Platt replies.

"No, you won't," Antoinette says, ready to kick us all out.

"Five minutes," Cassie says, "give them five minutes then you can focus on your patient."

"Three," Antoinette counters.

"Five," Elsbeth growls.

The tension in the room goes up about twelve notches and I look from one ripped badass to another. I have to wonder what damage Antoinette can do in a fight with her knowledge of anatomy.

"Five," Antoinette says finally, "then he rests."

"Deal," Elsbeth says, holding out her hand. "You shake when you make a deal. Greta taught me that. So shake, dammit."

"We're going to have to work on your social graces," Cassie says.

"*You're* gonna have to work on *your* social graces," Elsbeth replies.

"She learned that from Charlie," I say.

"Four minutes," Antoinette says.

"Right, the plan," I say. "We take the rafts and head downriver until we get to the River Arts district."

"That's pretty close to the interstate," Platt says. "The place will be crawling with Zs. Not to mention the wranglers."

"We're hoping for the Z part," John says, "not the wranglers so much."

"We'll goop up with Z guts," Reaper continues, "and work our way up Haywood Rd to downtown and the BB&T building. While the other half gets back into the rafts and floats ahead."

"To where the Bywater used to be," I say. "They wait for us there. That way we can push forward and not have to lose time doubling back. If we re-goop then we should be able to get through the Zs just fine."

"You're forgetting the human element," Platt says.

"We're not. I don't think the wranglers you saw are in the city," Stuart says. "The herds we ran into were running wild. My guess then? They are south driving the Zs forward to Asheville. Keeping them on track. They probably have strategic posts they're camped at to handle each wave being sent up from Atlanta."

"But you don't think they have a post downtown?" Platt asks.

"Why would they?" I say. "If the goal is to drive them into Asheville then there's no need for more wrangling."

"Who says their goal is just Asheville?" Cassie asks. "That's the weak part of the plan."

"Hardly the only one," Melissa snorts.

"So that's the first part," Platt nods, "what's the second?"

"You mean once we have communications up?" I ask then look at everyone else. "Well, we're going to have to play that by ear."

"At least until we know what everyone's status is," John says.

Platt shakes his head. "I don't like it."

"None of us do," Stuart responds, "but we can't sit here and wait to get overrun."

"That is unlikely," Cassie frowns.

"Listen, no offense," I say to her, "but it's inevitable. This estate is too big to keep locked down. Zs will find a way in. They always do. It's virtually guaranteed with the numbers we're dealing with."

"Okay, something's bothering me," Melissa says and everyone looks at her. "Let's say we are successful and get communications back up. Then we zip around and rescue every last person in Asheville." She holds out her hands. "Then what? Where do we go from there?"

"The Farm," I say. "At least, at first. It's big enough."

Melisa shakes her head as do John, Reaper and Platt. Stuart just looks at me.

"Okay," I sigh. "I know. Odds are the Farm is gone. It always attracted the largest number of Zs anyway because of the livestock. I know that. But where else do we have to go?"

That question hangs in the air as Antoinette stands and says, "Time's up. Get out."

***

"Great," Stella says. "We have a dump truck. Now what?"

Everyone sits close together inside what had been planned as the community clubhouse, but hadn't been fully finished before Z-Day hit. It looks like the new residents of Reynolds Mountain tried to fix it up with some paint, but really, it is just a large room with drywall and a concrete floor. Outside, a hundred yards down the mountain, the sound of the Zs at the gates continues. A monotonous drone of hunger that fills the air as the sun begins its slow climb from out behind the mountain.

Stella is standing before everyone as they huddle on the cold concrete, each looking miserable, hungry, distrustful.

"Where do we go?" Stella asks. "Whispering Pines is overrun. The Grove Park is gone."

"We don't know that," someone says.

"We don't know that it isn't," Lourdes responds, "and can't take the chance of getting stuck there if it is."

"Which still leaves the question of where to go," Stella repeats, "I'm open to suggestions."

"Doesn't sound like it," a woman mutters.

"What's that?" Stella snaps. "Speak up if you have something to say."

The woman stands and looks at Stella. "I said it doesn't sound like you're open to suggestions. Everything we say you shoot down. You're no better than Brenda is. Just another bitch wishing she had a dick."

"Hey!" Buzz shouts. "No need for that!"

The room explodes into arguments as people get to their feet, and in each other's face, and begin shouting and yelling. It's Whispering Pines versus Reynolds Mountain, civilian versus private military contractor.

"Stop it," Charlie says. "Stop it. Stop it! Stop it! STOP IT! STOPITSTOPITSTOPIT!"

He flies through the throng and starts randomly slapping people across the face. He doesn't care who he hits, so long as they shut the fuck up after he smacks them.

"I SAID STOP IT!" he screams at the top of his lungs.

The room goes quiet.

"Good," he says, "we go north."

They all stare at him.

He shakes his head and looks at everyone like they are idiots and his mother is not immune to the look.

"We can't go south because that's where the Zs are coming from," Charlie says now that he has everyone's attention. "We go north as far and fast as we can. Once we're clear of the Z herd we turn and head west. My dad told me that there are other places with people. He heard about somewhere out in the Plains, maybe."

"Kansas City," Greta says.

"Yeah, Kansas City," Charlie nods. "We load everyone up in that dump truck and we go north. Then west. And keep going until we are a long way from here."

"What'll we do for food?" someone asks.

"We'll have that same issue here," Charlie replies.

"What about the Farm?" another suggests.

Charlie looks over at Buzz. "No," the big man says, shaking his head. "The Zs had already taken Pierson Bridge. They'll be to the Farm about now. Even if it holds, we won't get through. Not with all the Zs the cows and pigs attract."

"North," Charlie says.

"Sweetie," Stella says, "it's not that easy."

"No shit, Mom," Charlie snaps. "Nothing is in this fucking world. I know most of you think kids like me and Greta have been sheltered from the worst since we were able to spend a few years in Whispering Pines." He holds up his hands and uses air quotes. "Because it was 'safe'." A hollow laugh bubbles up out of his throat. "But have you forgotten what we had to do before gates were built and fences put up?"

"Or after," Greta says, "in that fight cage. Or up on the Blue Ridge Parkway?"

"I don't sleep," Charlie says. "I doze a little, but I haven't had a full night's sleep since Z-Day. That was years ago. You know why? Because I lay awake, listening. I wait for the sounds of the Zs breaking through the fences, through the gates, breaking down our doors and coming up the stairs to fucking eat my face."

Everyone is silent, watching him closely.

"I'm sure most of you know how that feels," he continues. "I highly doubt I'm the only one that lies there in their bed knowing that the sheet and blanket draped across them won't do shit when the Zs break down the door." His voice catches and he falters.

Greta grabs his hand and squeezes it tight, giving him the strength to go on.

"There is no certainty in this world," he says. "There's no real safety. A lot of you do that thing adults do and just put on blinders and move forward. That's how you were raised. That's how you got through the old world of bills and shitty jobs and stupid politics and all that crap. But that shit doesn't fly anymore!

"You know what the best advice my dad ever gave me was? It was to keep your eyes open and look at the world because it can all be gone in a blink. Guess what, people? The world fucking blinked. It's over. So we keep going until we can't go any further."

"Farther," Greta says.

"It's further," Charlie counters.

"I don't think so," Greta frowns.

"Doesn't matter," Charlie smiles at her. "It sucks no matter what."

The room is filled with wet eyes and sniffles. Stella grabs onto her children and hugs them tightly.

"When did you get so grown up?" she asks Charlie.

"When the dead started eating people, Mom," he says.

"Duh," Greta adds.

***

The morning light hits the French Broad just as Critter drives the Jeep across the Fletcher Martin Rd Bridge up by Alexander. Dr. McCormick is passed out in the passenger seat, twitching and groaning as her brain tries to process the nightmare of the last twenty-four hours.

He taps the steering wheel with his fingers, drumming them in time with a wordless tune he's busy humming. The air around him begins to warm as the sun rises so he turns down the Jeep heat that blows on his feet. He's still humming when he comes to a four way stop. Normally he'd go straight and take Old Turkey Creek Rd up to New Leicester Highway then follow that all the way into the Pisgah National Forest. After a few turns on small roads named things like Panther Branch and Poplar Gap, he'd be just a few hidden twists from his holler.

Critter's holler: The place to be when trying to forget the Zs.

It was a motto he came up with when he decided to add a casino to the other illegal activities he provided. Not that anything is truly illegal anymore. Hard to break laws when there aren't any more laws to break. Or anyone to enforce them.

But Critter doesn't go straight to Old Turkey Creek Rd. Instead, he turns left and follows the winding country highway until he sees a rusted old gate off to his right. He stops the Jeep just in front and hops out, wincing as his knees protest and crack like gunshots.

"Ain't as spry as I used to be," he says then smiles as Dr. McCormick mutters back at him in her sleep.

The gate takes a little coaxing, but he gets it open, hops back into the Jeep, and drives up a barely perceptible, overgrown road.

It's really more of a glorified trail, but the Jeep fits, so he thinks of it as a road. It's a long climb uphill, and Critter gets slightly anxious about the amount of gas he's using, but he doesn't slow down, taking the twists and turns while barely touching the brakes.

When he gets to his destination, he shuts off the engine, grabs a pair of binoculars, and steps from the Jeep. He focuses the binoculars and smiles, even though most wouldn't smile at the sight below. But Critter isn't most, and his smiles aren't really smiles, more mischievous turns of his lips.

Asheville.

The city sits there in its mountain valley, with pillars of smoke coming from several locations as buildings burn, the streets overrun with Zs. Critter does a quick estimate as he scans the city and realizes there are easily ten thousand Zs moving about. Ten thousand that he can see. He gives out a low whistle.

"Everyone's dead, aren't they?" Dr. McCormick asks sleepily from back in the Jeep.

"No way to know," Critter says without taking the binoculars from his eyes. "But could be."

Then something catches his eyes and his smile of mischief turns to one of delight.

"Well, I'll be dipped in shit," he says.

"What?" Dr. McCormick asks.

Critter finally takes the binoculars away from his face and glances over his shoulder. Then looks quickly away.

"Sorry," he says.

"What?" Dr. McCormick says as she stands from peeing by the Jeep and pulls up her jeans. "Never seen a woman drop trou before?" She comes up to him and holds out her hand. "May I?"

"Yes, ma'am," Critter says as he hands over the binoculars.

"My, God," she says as she studies the almost endless numbers of Zs that fill the city.

"Now look down at the river," he says, "close to your two o'clock."

"My what?" Dr. McCormick asks. "Dammit Jim, I'm a doctor not a clock!"

"That's a good one," Critter chuckles. "I get that joke. Nice to have someone that knows things that happened before the internets turned it all to cats in damn shark costumes."

"I'll admit I liked that too," Dr. McCormick says. "Now stop making me hunt for it. Tell me what I'm looking for?"

But Critter doesn't need to.

"I'll also be dipped in shit," she laughs. "Is that who I think it is?"

"You know anyone else with a shiny spike for an arm?" Critter laughs. "Hard to miss that even from this distance."

Dr. McCormick hands him the binoculars. "So what does this mean?"

"Means we know someone we give a shit about is alive down there," Critter says. "And, as usual, the moron is heading *into* trouble, not away from it."

"Where are they going?" Dr. McCormick asks. "Why are they in rafts?"

"Best way to travel when the road's full of undead," Critter says.

"Now what?"

"I think they'll need a little help," Critter says.

"You have something that can help them? With all of those Zs?"

"Yes, ma'am, I do." Critter gives her a puzzled look. "Hold on now. Did you think I was just runnin' away?"

Dr. McCormick blushes.

"Well, I'll be," Critter says, nodding his head. "You don't have a very high opinion of me, do ya?"

"It's not that, Critter," Dr. McCormick replies. "No one really has a very high opinion of you. Except Jace, I think."

"Huh," Critter says, scratching the stubble on his chin. "Well, guess I best be provin' ya wrong then. Let's go."

"Where are we going?" she asks as they get back in the Jeep and Critter turns them around.

"Gonna swing by my place," Critter smiles. "Round up the gang." His smile widens. "And get my truck."

***

"What's wrong with you?" Elsbeth asks as we quietly paddle down the French Broad.

Or, as she quietly paddles. I forgot to bring my rafting adaptor for Stumpageddon. Right now, I'm sporting Mr. Spikey. Which everyone eyes nervously since one slip and I'll put a hole in the raft. The raft I'm floating in has Elsbeth, Melissa, What's-His-Name, and three sisters. That's one more than capacity, but I don't think it matters much. The second raft, close behind us, has Stuart, Reaper, John and three sisters. There are two kayaks leading the way, and one behind us, each with a sister. Antoinette and Stacy stayed behind with Platt.

I really wish I had a cooler of beers and some sunflower seeds to split and spit. That was kinda my floating thing pre-Z. Stella and I would take the kids down the French Broad in these tricked out tubes that could hold snacks and even had a built in cooler. That was the life.

The raft we're in is pretty sweet, and tricked out with fun things like holders for your rifles and straps so you can handcuff prisoners to the side, but it's just not the same as a nice blue and white tube on a Saturday afternoon. Unless today *is* Saturday. Is it? I can't fucking remember anymore.

"What do you mean?" I reply finally. "Nothing's wrong with me. I'm fine."

"You suck at lying," Elsbeth says. Melissa, up front, looks over her shoulder at us, but Elsbeth gives her a "fuck off" look. She shrugs and turns back around; everyone's used to Elsbeth's "fuck off" looks.

"I'm not lying," I say. Which is a lie, of course. I'm not fine. My shoulder is about to send me over the edge. "I'm just tired."

"I'm tired too," Elsbeth says, "but I'm still me. You aren't being you."

Okay...I'm confused.

"Okay, I'm confused," I say. It's better to say the words out loud. "What are you talking about?"

"The Long Pork I rescued had funny pink pants on and a butterfly shirt," Elsbeth says. "You were going to be eaten, but you were funny at it."

143

"Thanks," I say, "I try to keep it light in the apocalypse."

"See," she nods, "that's funny. But it's not enough."

"El, just come out and say it," I plead. "I'm not following you."

"No, you ain't," she says. "You're in the raft with me. How could you follow me if you are right here? Stop being stupid and answer me."

"I can't answer you if I don't know what you are talking about!" I snap.

"Shhhh," one of the sisters scolds. I think it's a Tracy. Or a Lacy. Right, because Stacy is back at the Biltmore. I think. I don't know. I'm too afraid to ask. They get a tad irritated when I don't know their names.

"Just tell me what you mean," I whisper to Elsbeth.

"You were funny," she says. "You made me laugh. When me and Pa had you all trussed up you were making me laugh."

"Oh, was that what I was doing?" I say. "And here I thought my comedy routine didn't go over well because of all the pissing in my pants I did."

"That's funny," one of the sisters observes.

"Thanks," I say. "See? I'm still funny."

"No, you aren't," Elsbeth says. "You're being funny now because you don't want to answer me. So answer me, Long Pork. What's wrong with you?"

About fifty sarcastic comments go through my head. Things like:

"We don't have enough time in the day to explain everything wrong with me."

Or:

"Oh, nothing, just enjoying a float on the way to my doom."

Or, the perennial favorite of all teenagers:

"Nothing. What's wrong with *you*?"

I have a ton more, but none of them come out of my mouth. What does come out surprises even me.

"I'm scared," I say. "With every day I get more and more scared. Petrified."

"Once I was afraid, I was petrified," a sister starts to hum.

"Good one," I smile. "But I've tried the Gloria Gaynor therapy and I still don't feel like I'll survive."

"We're all scared," Elsbeth says.

"Oh, I know that intellectually," I say, tapping my head. "But that's the problem. I'm intellectually terrified. Ever since Mondello dropped the bomb about the Consortium and there being other places like that, I haven't slept worth a shit."

"Then suck it up, Long Pork," she says, "stop being scared."

"I've tried," I protest. "I'm usually really good at burying things deep down and locking them away for later. But here's the problem, El, now *is* that later."

She frowns at me.

"Do you get what I'm saying?" I ask. "The vault of Jace is all full. I gots terrors leaking out my ears."

"No, you don't," she says, obviously checking out my ears.

"It's a saying," a sister says, "he doesn't mean he actually..."

"I know," Elsbeth growls, "I'm not the stupid one. He is."

"You wanted to know what's wrong with me and that's it," I say. "My mind is working overtime on the Consortium issue. I can't think straight half the time. I haven't come up with a great idea or inspiration in months."

"You've been doing great with the Whispering Pines rebuild," Melissa says.

"That's just robot work," I say and hold up a finger to Elsbeth. "Yes, I know we don't have robots. What I mean is I don't have to think to use a hammer. I don't have to think to stack boards. I don't even have to think when we're rebuilding a house. There are plenty of people better at that than me. I just grab some wood and nails and get to work."

"What are you talking about?" Melissa asks. "You improved the gates."

"No, I didn't," I admit, "that was Charlie and Greta. I was stuck and they started brainstorming."

Melissa shakes her head. "You ripped off your kids' ideas? Have you no shame?"

"Ha ha," I smirk. "What else was I going to do? People look to me to be the Big Brain of Whispering Pines. When all I want to be is the Curled Up in a Fetal Position Brain of Whispering Pines."

"Anxiety," Elsbeth says. "Greta taught me that word. She says I have it and it's why I don't relax like normal people."

"Just a wild guess here," I say, "but I'm going with it's the captured by a canny and also being a trained killer element that makes it hard to relax."

Elsbeth glares. "Anxiety."

"Got it. Anxiety," I agree. "My bad."

"That's what you have," Elsbeth nods. "You need to close your eyes and go to your quiet place."

I stare at her.

"I'm sorry, but did you just tell me to go to my 'quiet place'?"

"Yes."

"And you have been doing this? Going to your quiet place?"

"No."

"I'm confused," I sigh.

"I don't have a quiet place," Elsbeth says. "No place to go. All noise."

She smacks herself in the side of the head like she used to do when I first found her. Or she found me. Whatever, we'll share the credit.

"Don't do that," I say quietly.

"You have a quiet place," she says, pointing a finger at me.

"No, I don't think so," I say, "not anymore. It got hacked off along with my arm."

"That's crap," Melissa says. "You still have Stella and the kids. Use that."

"But they are the problem!" I snap and then quiet down as I receive several angry glares. "Sorry. Stella and the kids are the fuel to it all. Look at me. Look at my arm. I'm in no shape to keep them safe. You've seen me fight with this thing. I'm slow and I'm nowhere near as effective as I used to be. I'm a liability to them and to everyone."

"Oh, boo hoo and whaa whaa," Elsbeth says, rubbing her fingers together. "Know what this is?"

"The world's smallest violin," I answer. "Yeah, I know that one."

She looks at her fingers then at me. "No, it's me squishing your tiny dick because you are being such a pussy," she snorts. "Why would you think it's a violin? I don't play violin."

"Right, sure, my bad," I reply. "Got it. It's you crushing my tiny, Hey!"

"Long Pork," Stuart hisses from the other raft. "Shut the fuck up or I'll swim over there and shut you the fuck up."

"She started it," I mutter.

"Pull your balls out of your ass and be Long Pork again," Elsbeth says. "You could die today. Don't die being stupid. Die funny."

She nods at me like she just gave me the sagest advice ever spoken in the history of sage advice.

And, admittedly, she's not that far off.

"Okay," I say, "I'll try."

"Do or do not," the sisters say in unison, "there is no try."

"I don't get it," Elsbeth frowns.

"It's from a movie," I say. "If we live I'll show it to you."

"Can I have popcorn?" Elsbeth asks. "I always eat popcorn when I watch movies with Greta and Charlie. Always."

There's a slight hint of menace in her voice. Elsbeth takes her popcorn very seriously, apparently.

"All the popcorn you can eat," I nod.

"We're here," John says as the rafts start to paddle towards the shore.

We get to the riverbank and have to struggle to keep the rafts from getting away from us. The sisters in the kayaks start tying lines to the rafts and get ready to tow them down to our rendezvous point downriver where the Bywater used to be.

I miss sitting by the river there with a cold pint of porter and a summer breeze blowing across my bald scalp. At one point, someone had tried to make a go of the place, but it just wasn't a secure enough area. Too close to I-26. The Zs would just tumble over the railing and swarm down at them. Stuart told me he found the fools massacred there with coals in the barbecues still warm and empty beer cans everywhere. At least they went out with a party.

Everyone scrambles up the riverbank, grabbing on to tree roots and rocks for leverage. I don't really have quite the same abilities anymore, so when I grab with my good hand, it slips on some moss and I almost tumble backwards into the French Broad. Instinctively I jam Stumpageddon's spike into the wet earth. Then I choke on a scream.

I do a pretty good job of that scream choking. Turning my head, I act like it's a cough I'm trying to keep quiet. I get some glances and just nod and smile. Then make my way up the bank and out onto the shoulder of Riverside Dr.

For once, my major source of pain isn't Stumpageddon. It's my shoulder. It's getting worse and worse. I honestly have no idea how much longer I can take it. Or fake it. This isn't a secret that I'll be able to keep forever. At some point, I'll have to tell them. Every minute I keep my friends in the dark is a minute closer to me becoming….well…you know.

Jesus, is this how I go out? Fucking fuck fuck.

For now, I have to play it off and act like the pussy boy missing an arm and not the pussy boy about to get a hankering for friend flesh.

We crouch at the edge of Riverside Dr, hiding in a runoff ditch thick with vegetation. The pain goes way past eleven as Stuart comes up and slaps me on the shoulder.

"You up for this?" he asks. "Your cannibal savant hasn't rattled your cage too much, has she?"

"I'm good, I'm good," I whisper. "This isn't my first apocalypse, you know."

"You've survived other apocalypses then?" Stuart asks, his eyebrows raising.

"No, I mean it isn't my first life or death situation," I snap.

"I know what you meant," Stuart says. "Relax. I need your head in the game for this. We'll be relying on you to help disable the jammer."

"Me? Why me?"

"Because of the brain," Stuart says, tapping me on the forehead.

"I'm trained in advanced electronics," Steph says. "I can disable it. We won't need him."

"See?" I say. "You don't need me."

Don't need me.

Not with the Uber Girls around.

Maybe that's it. Maybe it's not that I'm scared, but that I feel like a redundancy.

Before Lourdes and her crew came to town, I was the top guy with the ideas. If it needed to be figured out then I found a way to figure it out. But then Joe T and Shumway were on the scene, making it very obvious I wasn't going to be the one getting Asheville's infrastructure up and going. They had that handled.

And security? Lourdes and her Team were way more capable. Anything I came up with they could poke holes through until I gave up.

I gave up.

Wow. Is that the kernel of truth I've been hiding from myself?

"Jace!" Stuart hisses, looking back at me as I see everyone scrambling out of the ditch and into the road. "Fucking move!"

"Sorry, sorry," I say. "You know me and my space cadet ways."

"I do," Stuart says as we dash across the road to a massive pile of bricks that used to be where a new set of condos was going to be built. "Knock it the fuck off."

I give him a thumbs up. With the only thumb I have.

God, listen to me! Could I be any more of a whiny bitch?

Ha, that makes me think of the show Friends. You know the one where they call out Chandler for the way he puts the emphasis on *be* every time he'd say something. Which, of course, makes me think of the couch episode.

Pivot! Pivot! Pivot!

"What the fuck?" John says.

Everyone is staring at me.

Fuck...was that out loud?

"Fuck," I say. "Was that out loud?" I can tell by the looks on their faces it was. "Sorry."

"Zs," Cassie says. "I count eighty. Coming this way."

I only count sixty, but I'm slipping so... Oh, she means those other twenty shambling out of that warehouse. Yeah, I saw those. What? I did!

We don't ask why, just start sprinting up the hill towards downtown. As we pass Clingman Ave, and Dehlia joins us, I look over and see why she's booking ass.

That small group of Zs multiplied. Into a very, very large group of Zs. I knew it was too fucking easy so far!

The roar of a thousand moans fills the air as they catch sight of our group.

Feets don't fail me now!

CHAPTER SEVEN

The Jeep rolls to a stop and Critter puts a finger to his lips. Dr. McCormick gives him a puzzled look, but he just smiles and shakes his head. He quietly gets out and tiptoes his way down the dirt road, crouched low. It takes her minute to figure out what he reminds her of, but then she gets it: the Grinch. Critter looks like the Grinch sneaking along to steal all the Whoville Christmas presents.

But why is he sneaking? She'd get out and follow, but there is only a foot of road on her side before it takes a sudden drop of about 500 feet. She has a feeling Critter did that on purpose since the road is plenty wide. Wide enough in fact to drive two large trucks on side by side.

"I ain't asleep, Critter," a man's voice grumbles. "Hard to sleep when you come tearing up the road in that thing."

Dr. McCormick jumps at the voice, searching the road and the surroundings for the source. Then she sees him, sitting against a large oak up the road. He's dressed in camouflage gear from head to toe and blends right in with foliage at the base of the tree.

"Shit," Critter says, "thought I had you that time, Red."

"Ain't nobody can sneak up on me," the man says as he stands and tilts a cowboy hat back on his head. Even the cowboy hat is camo.

The man holds out his hand and Critter shakes it vigorously. Looking past Critter, the man named Red spots Dr. McCormick and nods, tipping his hat to her.

"Ma'am," he says.

"Come on," Critter says, turns, and walks back to the Jeep. "Meet the lady doctor."

"Howdy," Red says when they get to the Jeep. "Pleasure. Are you really a lady doctor or just a doctor that's a lady?"

This puzzles her for a second until she realizes what he's asking. "Oh, no, I'm not a gynecologist. I'm actually, or was, a proctologist."

"Oh," Red nods, "a butthole doctor. Well, medicine is medicine."

"Red here is my guard dog," Critter says. "He stays out here night and day. And no matter how hard I try I never catch him sleeping."

The man is tall and Dr. McCormick can see that he's muscular. Maybe mid-forties with a little bit of grey stubble showing from under his hat. But it's the large splotch of red across his left cheek that's his most distinguishing feature.

"You looking at my beauty mark?" Red smiles.

"Sorry," Dr. McCormick says. "Occupational hazard. It's actually called a port-wine..."

"Nevus flammeus," Red interrupts. "But, yeah, it's also called a port-wine stain. I'm well aware."

"I didn't mean to offend you," Dr. McCormick apologizes.

"None taken," Red smiles. "I just like to show off."

"Red has a PhD," Critter grins, "in assholery."

"Comparative literature," Red nods.

"Oh, wow," Dr, McCormick says, surprised. "I didn't know UNCA offered that."

"I didn't either," Red says, "that's why I got mine at Cornell."

"Oh," she says, her face turning almost as red as the mark on Red's cheek.

"See," Critter nods, "Assholery."

"What's with the ride?" Red asks. "Thought you were keeping that in town."

"Circumstances done changed," Critter says and fills Red in on the details.

"Holy wow," Red says, shaking his head. "Big Daddy? Dead? That's just gonna be more bad news for your nephew."

"My nephew?" Critter asks. "Which one?"

"Gunga," Red replies. "Got here last night with a handful of folks from the Farm. Said the place had been overrun. I didn't believe it at first so I sent a couple guys to check it out. Now I know why they haven't come back."

"Who'd you send?"

"Malcolm and Whitey."

"Those two? They'd get themselves killed picking blueberries."

"Which is why I sent them and not any of the good ones," Red says. "We can spare those morons."

"That's horrible," Dr. McCormick says. "Two men have probably lost their lives and you talk about them as if they were just chickens waiting to be slaughtered."

Critter and Red look at her, look at each other then look back at her.

"So?" they say together.

"Sick," she says and leans into her seat. "Are we sitting here all day or what?"

"I like her," Red says, "and she's right. What's up, Critter? You could have just driven right past."

"I need you to take the lady doctor into the holler proper," Critter says and hooks a thumb up over his shoulder. "I'm gonna hoof it and pick up my truck."

"Oh," Red nods, "not feeling it today, Crit."

"I don't care," Critter says. "I need you to do this. Take her in, fetch her some food and let her get cleaned up, then sit tight until I get there."

"Nope," Red says, "not today."

Critter sighs and rubs his face. "Listen…"

"Nope."

"Dammit, Red!" Critter yells. "Ain't no time for your craziness! I give you a lot of leeway 'round here, but right now, right this very minute, I am all out of leeway!"

Red leans his hand against the hood of the Jeep, careful to keep his body clear of the blades. He drums his fingers over and over and over.

up, are platforms with buildings made from various materials. Walkways of wood and steel connect the buildings, which as they drive closer, look like trailers and modular houses.

"How did you get them up there?" Dr. McCormick asks.

"Crane," Critter replies, but doesn't elaborate.

They turn to the left and pull up next to a long row of vehicles.

"End of the line, doc," Critter says. "Let's go get us some food and a shower. Not together mind you, I ain't that kind of guy." Critter chuckles. "You can rest up for an hour or so. It'll take Red a bit to get the truck."

"What's so important about this truck?" she asks as she gets out and stretches.

Critter just smiles.

***

"I thought we were going to gunk up before taking on the Zs!" I yell as we sprint up Haywood Rd towards Hilliard Ave. "Wasn't that the plan?"

"Still is!" Cassie yells back from the front of the group. "Just going to do it on the fly!"

On the fly? What the hell does that mean?

Oh, I see…

We get to Hilliard Ave and turn right, which points us to the heart of Asheville. But we aren't the only ones thinking about taking a leisurely stroll through downtown. A good few hundred Zs have decided to take in the sights. The herd covers the entire street, from sidewalk to sidewalk, and up over into the parking lots and yards of the businesses and former residences.

Cassie and the sisters don't even hesitate, they just wade in, blades out, and start hacking. They've cut a fifteen foot swath of destruction before the rest of us even get to the edge of the herd.

"Here's your gunk," Elsbeth says as she reaches down and scoops out a handful of putrid guts from a fallen Z. She slaps it onto my head and starts mushing it around. "Close your eyes, stupid."

Yeah, I didn't really need to be told that, but I nod anyway and close my eyes. The smell is beyond disgusting. But, being a modern man post-Z, I take it and deal. She splats more onto my chest and arms. I wince and almost cry out when she smacks a gob of guts onto my shoulder.

"There," she says as she grabs my right arm (the upper part of course) and pulls me down the street right into the throng of undead. I open my eyes and catch her watching me. "You're hurt worse than you said."

She looks at the half-arm she's holding and gives it a tug.

FUCKING BITCH!

I don't say that outloud, but it's obvious it shows on my face. I can feel pain sweat start to slicken the already slick Z guts on my forehead. The shit's gonna drip in my eyes soon. Fun!

Pausing only to give me that knowing cannibal savant look of hers, Elsbeth scoops up some Z guts for herself and smears the offal all over her body. With one hand since she won't let go of my arm with the other. I look about and see the rest of our group gunking up, while the sisters keep cutting, chopping, and hacking through the herd. I start to worry they'll get attacked because they didn't stop to get covered in the sweet, sweet innards of our zombie overlords.

But with the damage they are doing, they don't need to stop. I can see black blood and flesh dripping off their ever-moving bodies. They are like a fucking Cuisinart made of arms and legs and lady parts. And steel. Plenty of steel. But someone forgot to put the lid on that food processor and shit is spraying everywhere.

Man, using a food prep metaphor is making me fucking hungry. Even with the stench I'm covered in. When was the last time I fucking ate?

"OW!" I yell as Elsbeth gives my arm an extra squeeze.

"Stop dreaming," she says and finally lets go, pushing me forward. "Act dead."

The Zs are attracted to the movement of the sisters ahead, but confused by their smell. Some look towards me, eager to investigate the new kid in school, but none take more than a casual step in my direction before their nostrils inform them I'm one of the gang.

I do my best Z impression and stagger and stumble my way along Hilliard. Loud groans from behind make me look over my shoulder (the one not fucking killing me!) and I see the River Arts herd coming up behind us. More fun!

But I keep it calm; keep it cool. I'm a cucumber on the wind!

The problem with pretending to be a Z is that you can't show pain. You can't, say, get your shoulder that is festering with Z death slammed into over and over by a fuck ton of uncaring, unfeeling, and, if I do say so, *rude* Zs then be all like "Ow, knock it off!" Can't do that. What you can do is hiss and groan right along with them. Which, and this may sound strange, is actually quite liberating. It's a strange type of stress release even when not trying to hide the fact you and agony are shaking hands.

Okay, maybe *shaking hands* isn't the best metaphor for me to use.

My groans need a little work, but my hisses are top notch. The only problem is I seem to be getting the Zs riled up around me. They aren't quite as docile as they should be. Every time air escapes between my teeth because I'm about to scream, a Z cocks its head in my direction. I don't know if it senses my life giving livingness or if it's just a fan of my sibilant techniques.

I can see the sisters getting farther and farther away, shoving and fighting through the herd, making it easier for the rest of us to keep going with a bit more elbow room. Elsbeth pushes past me and I cringe, thinking I don't have anyone at my back. But with a casual stutter-step and a twist of my neck, I can see that guy there. You know the one with the body armor and the rifle? Fuck...uh. Shit, you know, what's his name? That guy.

Whatever his name is he gives me a look like I'm an idiot then nods. I nod back. He barely shakes his head no, which still attracts some attention, then nods again. I nod back. Just like before. I'm not sure what his issue is. I'm giving him the bro, "Whassup?" nod. That's still cool post-Z, right? I didn't miss a bro memo or something did I? I've been out of the pop culture social norms loop for a few years. Maybe he's coming on to me? Not that there's anything wrong with that. I mean, I'm all about Team Stella, but if he needs to feel loved then...

Slam!

Ow.

Oh, he was nodding at the lamppost I was shuffling towards.

The skin on my forehead splits wide open and fresh blood starts to poor down my face. Fuck. I can barely see with the sweat and goop and now this shit? I can tell I really fucked myself up as I take a few steps back. But I have the presence of mind not to cry out. I let out a snarly groan then a small hiss for good measure. I'm just one of the Zs here. Move along, undead, move along, nothing to see.

But, as I've mentioned before, eyesight isn't their go to sense. Smell is number one in their book. And right now, I smell like a dipshit with fresh, delicious blood dripping from his eyebrows. Mmmmmm, blood…

The mood of the Z herd changes instantly. Where there was blind marching, and confusion with the sisters up ahead, there is now raging hunger and directed aggression. And that aggression is directed at said idiot that is always too busy thinking about the next step instead of watching where that next step leads.

The world slows down.

Up ahead I see hunks of Zs flying here and there as the sisters chop, chop, chop merrily along their way. I can see sunlight glinting off the oil that coats Elsbeth's hair because she hasn't had a shower in days. It's kind of cool. I watch as John and Reaper turn towards me, their eyes wide with shock, their mouths set in a determined grimace that tells me I fucked it all up. A sound finds my ears, but it's so far off, like a distant echo you can't place in the night.

Then there are the Zs.

Each bit of decayed flesh and tattered cloth is outlined in a bright aura. Grey flaps of skin flutter lazily from broken jaws and exposed cheekbones. Hands that are nothing but splintered bone and leather tight sinew start to lift towards me. Teeth of various shapes and sizes begin to make themselves seen from behind shredded lips. Moans and groans, hisses and snarls are a steady drumbeat in my brain as the volume slowly, slowly, slowly starts to ratchet up until…

"LONG PORK!" Elsbeth screams.

No more slomo. The world slams back into real time.

Spinning and shoving, I try to make some room in the encroaching horde of Zs. They can smell that special Jace spice that brings all the Zs to my yard. Despite the pain, I bring Stumpageddon up and slam Mr. Spikey into an eye socket. I yank back and hit another Z then another and another. But we all know what is going to happen, don't we? The numbers are too great. I am like a dead nutria tossed into a gator pit to entertain the fat tourists.

Not that fat tourists exist anymore. Or maybe they do. As far as I know there's some oblivious family from Wisconsin still putzing around the country in their Ford minivan and hitting all the roadside attractions. I'd love to do that some day. Just pick up and leave with the Fam and go see that biggest ball of twine or the Cadillac graveyard. I bet the lines aren't very long these days.

But, enough about my travel plans, I should really be thinking about the Zs that are very close to pulling me to the ground.

Stumpageddon slams home over and over while I use my intact arm (don't have a name for that guy, but I'm taking suggestions) swings wide as I try to push the Zs back. Gunk or no gunk, these guys smell blood and they are coming in for the kill. Stealth time is over, quiet time is up, it's boom stick time! Or boom twig time since I don't have a boom stick and only have a 9mm at my hip that John gave me.

I pull the pistol and fire into one skull then another. Black blood and rotten brains fill the air. I'm glad my slomo time is done because no one wants to see that shit splatter through the air at 6 frames per second. That's just John Woo overkill right there.

Hands have me and I'm going down. Stumpageddon is keeping the fuckers back enough that I can get a couple more shots in. Then just as I pull the trigger, a Z grabs my arm. The shot goes wide.

"Fucker!" John screams. "You almost fucking shot me!"

Good thing that Z grabbed me. I guess I didn't notice that John had waded in; I just about blew his head off.

Gunfire erupts everywhere and Zs start falling. I empty my pistol and then use it as a club as John pulls on my shoulder, rescuing me from the mosh pit of death. Reaper has his M-4 on full auto and is cutting Zs out at the legs. In fact, as I look around, I see everyone doing that. The sisters, Elsbeth, Stuart, Melissa, Reaper, that guy, all shooting or cutting the legs out from under the Zs. They aren't going for kill shots as much as incapacitation shots.

Soon there is a makeshift alleyway of Zs we can hurry through. The piles of crippled undead keep the still mobile ones from overrunning us. John has his hand at the small of my back and is shoving me forward so all I really do is concentrate on my footing and stay moving, making sure I don't fuck up worse by stumbling.

There's a loud whistle and I can see Cassie up ahead moving left onto Lexington Ave. The sisters all turn in perfect unison, creating this whirling dervish of slicing and dicing. They ripple around each other, seamlessly working together in an ever moving killing machine. My brain is quickly confused by what my eyes see. There are almost too many blades moving for the amount of hands up there. And where did they get all the blades? I know I saw some knives on the young women, but where did they get all those short swords and machetes and shit? Did they always have them? Man, my observation skills have gone down the crapper.

"Knock it off!" Elsbeth yells, suddenly at my elbow. Where'd John go? Oh, he's with Reaper and Melissa keeping the Zs from climbing up over their fallen comrades. Sidestepping at a dangerous pace, they move along the line, blasting anything that moves. Heads explode, chests burst open, Zs fall, collapsing across the borders and adding to the volume.

But there are so many of them. Thousands of undead crammed into the tight space of Asheville's city streets. And they are fucking hungry.

"Down!" Elsbeth shouts and shoves the top of my head towards the ground.

I barely catch a glimpse of a head spinning off to my right as her arm moves with unseen speed. A body rolls over the top of the Z pile and thumps into my legs. The fuckers are figuring out that we aren't going to come to them; they have to come to us. So despite the best laid plans and all that, the Z alley we are hustling through has become a Z gauntlet as putrid arms reach for us and the faster of the undead start to tumble over the sides. If this keeps up we'll be trapped in minutes.

But we don't stop. Gunfire is everywhere and black blood is raining down on us as Elsbeth leaps and turns, bringing her blades home with every swipe. We are now moving slowly up Lexington Ave, only four blocks from the BB&T building. So I focus on that.

But the cosmos finds me lacking and it's all over before it began.

"FUUUUUUUUUUUCK!" I scream as I roll onto my side, my hand clutching at my shoulder. "FUUUUUUUCK!"

Elsbeth and John pull me to my feet and keep me going. We are so close, but I'm already done. There's no way I'm raising Stumpageddon again. I can barely think let alone attack or defend. Every footstep is one of will power and concentration.

"Leave me!" I cry, knowing I'm slowing them down. "I'm already dead! Go!"

"Fuck you!" Elsbeth snarls as she severs a Z head. "Keep walking!"

"John! You have to go on without me!" I shout.

"Not happening, LP!" he yells back. "We don't leave men behind!"

"Frag!" Stuart yells and I don't even have time to react before an explosion sends Z parts raining down on us.

He yells it again and again and we follow the path of destruction. Behind us, just down the block is a blood curdling scream that is cut short. We all know what that means.

I'm sure silent prayers are said, but we don't have the luxury of bowing our heads in respect. That'll come later, if there is a later.

"There!" Cassie yells and points with one of her blades as it drips black goo. "That door!"

We are at the intersection of Patton and Lexington and just across from us is the back entrance to the BB&T building, the tallest building in Asheville. I hope that the jammer is up there and all of this hasn't been a massive waste of time. And waste of life.

With a final push, our group cuts and shoots its way through the Zs to a glass door that has been smashed in.

"Behind us!" Cassie yells as the women create a protective half-circle between the Zs and us.

There are no rookies in the apocalypse. You become seasoned pros at knowing when to move forward and when to fall back. You also become good at knowing when either of those options aren't going to work. It's the art of the sidestep. Which we employ on three, two, one.

"Zs!" John yells as he opens fire on the horde that is crammed inside the lobby of the BB&T building.

Smears of blood and chunks of flesh cover the beige tile. The Zs were obviously baited into filling the large space, a deliberate attempt to use the undead as a barrier.

"Up here!" Stuart yells as he yanks open the door to the stairs. Zs spill out, but he's ready for them, letting them fall past as he opens fire.

The stairway is dark, but I can see heads explode as each muzzle flash illuminates the space for a split second. Stuart dodges to the side as the Zs lunge at him. We swoop in behind to take care of them. Heads are split or severed, decayed faces kicked in, reaching hands lopped off. We kick and shove past the gnashing teeth and follow Stuart as he takes point. I'm suddenly in the center behind that one guy with Reaper, Melissa and John behind me.

But I'm quickly shoved out of the way as Melissa moves past, handing Stuart a newly loaded pistol whenever he reaches back, switching it out for his empty one. Then I'm at the back with John as Reaper moves in and provides backup with Melissa. I'm John's eyes, making sure he doesn't trip over the fallen bodies of the Zs that litter the stairs. He steps agilely over the corpses even though he's walking backwards up the stairs, keeping the few Zs that get past Elsbeth and the sisters from bum rushing us.

Then "I'm out!" Stuart shouts.

There's some more last gunfire and soon all I hear is thunk and thud, whack and smack. I say hear because without the muzzle flashes, the stairway becomes a pitch black hell of Z snarls and human grunts. It's all I can do to keep from falling flat on my face, let alone help John up the steps. But luckily, there are enough corpses strewn across the stairs to slow down any undead pursuers. John slings his rifle and he is quickly leading *me* up the stairs.

The Zs thin out as we get higher and higher, which is good because we slow down considerably with every floor we gain. No one says it, but this is our last push. Once we get to the roof, we had better find the jammer because we aren't up for a new scavenger hunt. It's all I can do to put one foot in front of the other and scrape my boots along the edges of each step. I'm climbing with my hand on the railing as much as with my legs.

"Door," Stuart gasps. I hear him rattle the knob. "Locked.

"Got it," the guy says. There's some movement as Stuart and what's his name switch places. Then I hear scraping of metal on metal, a loud whack, and the clang of the door handle hitting the floor. "There."

Daylight streams in from where the handle was and in that light I can see the PC guy crouched by the door, a cutting tool and hammer in his hands. Good thing he had that in his pack. It looks like a handy rig and I make a mental note to ask him about it later. More of those would be good for the scavengers to have on hand.

But I don't get a chance to ask him.

A muzzle pushes through the other side of the door and fires. The guy's face rips right off as more than a few bullets tear into his head. Stuart reacts immediately, drawing his machete and bringing it down onto the muzzle. There's a cry of pain from the other side of the door and the muzzle slips from view. Stuart must have hit the gun hard enough to send a shock wave up the fucker's arm, like when you ding a baseball wrong with an aluminum bat. That shit fucking hurts.

Then shit gets even more strange. I have no idea why I do it, but something comes over me. Maybe it's the sight of a man's eyeballs disintegrating or watching bits of his teeth explode from his mouth. Maybe it's because we have been fighting Zs for so long that human on human violence shocks me. Maybe it's just my time to lose my shit completely.

"JEFF!" I scream, finally remembering the guy's name, and reach for the door. I yank it open and burst out onto the roof. "YOU FUCK!"

A man is crouched right there, shaking one hand as he reaches for a rifle at his feet with his other hand. I jam Mr. Spikey into his head, but miss his eye and instead rip his cheek to shreds. It may have been a mis-stab, but it does the trick. The man screams and his free hand goes to his face, giving me time to get in closer. My fist meets his temple and he crumples. Then I have the rifle up one handed and I just start firing, screams of rage exploding from my throat.

I empty the magazine, but keep screaming until I feel hands on my shoulders, shaking me, yelling at me to shut he fuck up because it's all over.

"It is?" I ask, looking into Stuart's face.

"You killed them," he nods and takes the rifle from me. "The roof is clear."

"Them?" I look about and see three more bodies on the roof, all lying in quickly spreading pools of blood. They are human corpses, not Zs. I just blew away three living men.

The first man at my feet starts to groan and John grabs him by the collar and drags him over to his buddies.

"See that?" he says. "You want to be next?"

"Fuck...you," the man grunts.

John drags him over to the short wall at the edge of the building and then pushes. The man's top half starts to go over, but John grips the guy's belt, holding him securely enough so he waivers at the precipice.

"See all that down there?" John says. "You go over and odds are the fall will kill you. But then again maybe it won't. Maybe that herd of Zs will cushion your fall just enough to keep you alive, in excruciating pain, while they rip you apart and eat you alive."

"I lay ten on he dies in the fall," Melissa says.

"Ten says he doesn't," Stuart says. "Those Zs are squishy."

"Where's the jammer?" John asks.

"Fuck you," the man says. "You won't keep me alive even if I tell you."

"Hey, John?" I say, smiling. "Would that be it?"

Next to a row of old satellite TV dishes is a large black case. Miscellaneous wires stream out from the case and plug directly into the dozens of dishes. Next to the case is another one with a bank of solar panels on top of it.

"That's it," John says and let's go. The man's screams get quieter and quieter until we hear a thud way down below.

"Well then?" Stuart asks.

John looks casually over the edge and nods. "Squishy enough."

A cry of pain echoes up to us then stops.

I hurry (I use that word lightly) over to the jammer and take a look at all the wires coming from the first case. Then I look at the second case.

"Nice battery pack," I say and disconnect the cord going from it to the black case. I look up at Stuart. "You think that Steph chick is gonna be pissed I took the glory?"

"I think she'll be pissed if you call her a chick," Stuart warns.

We don't have to wait for long before chimes, rings, and buzzes emit from our pockets. We have Wi-Fi!

Then my phone rings. It doesn't buzz like I have a text, but actually rings. Well, it not so much rings as starts playing Sweet Caroline. Not the Neil Diamond version, but the live Elvis Presley version. Because it's The King singing Neil. That was my pre-Z bliss.

"You going to answer that then?" Stuart asks as I stare at my phone.

My screen says "UNKOWN" across it, which pre-Z I would have let go to voicemail. But I'm pretty sure voicemail doesn't exist anymore. In fact, I have no idea how a call is even happening.

"Yello?" I say as I answer the call. "This is Jason Stanford."

"Please hold, Mr. Stanford," a voice says.

"Uh…okay," I reply then pull the mic away from my face a little and smile at the others. "I'm on hold."

"You're what?" Stuart asks, his face a mix of shock and rage. "Who the fuck would…"

But I don't hear the rest of what he asks.

"Hello, Mr. Stanford," a woman greets me. "It's a pleasure finally to speak with you. You are a busy, busy man up there in Asheville."

"Yeah, I'm rarely bored," I say. "Uh, who do I have the pleasure of speaking with?"

"With whom," the woman corrects me. "Not who."

"Fuck you," I respond. "Whomever you are."

"You are as sarcastic as the reports say," the woman continues. "Let's hope you are just as intelligent."

"Lady, I really don't have time for banter with a mysterious bad guy right now, okay? Get to the fucking point and tell me who you are and how the fuck we are talking on a cell phone!"

"The technology doesn't matter," she says. "It's not as hard as you think. As for who I am, well, that's easy. My name is Camille Thornberg. I believe you know my daughter Carly. Or, as you refer to her, Elsbeth."

"Oh…fuck," I say.

"Oh fuck indeed, Mr. Stanford," Camille laughs. "Do I have your undivided attention now?"

"Undividedly," I say.

CHAPTER EIGHT

Several men shove the gates wide then sprint back to the dump truck that is already rolling past them. They grab on to anything they can and climb up into the bed with the rest of the Whispering Pines refugees and Reynolds Mountain residents. Tension and rivalry is still there as the two factions subconsciously keep space between them, but that rivalry is quickly forgotten as the dump truck speeds past the gates and into the waiting throng of Zs.

The truck slams into the Zs and black blood and gore spray up from the tires, splashing across everyone in the bed. There are cries of disgust at first, but they dwindle as the dump truck keeps moving, and the gore keeps splashing. Gunfire is heard from the Humvees riding behind the dump truck as Lourdes and her PCs take out the Zs coming out of the woods at the truck as it winds its way down to Merrimon Ave.

Stella, riding in front with Buzz driving, points at the street below. Charlie and Greta are seated between the two, their mouth hanging open at the sight.

"We can't stop," she says. "If we do we'll get swarmed."

"I know," Buzz says.

"And that's a sharp turn," Stella says.

"I know," Buzz replies.

"You take it too fast and we'll roll!" Stella shouts as they get to the turn.

"I know, Stella!" Buzz yells. "Back off!"

He cranks the wheel at the last possible second and the dump truck barrels into the herd of Zs that fill the street. The shocks and suspension groan with the momentum and for a split second, it feels as if the right side wheels will actually lift off the ground, but Buzz slams the accelerator home and the force of motion corrects the vehicle and all wheels stay grounded.

"Phew," Stella says, "good driving."

"Thanks," Buzz nods, "but this is far from over."

Stella gasps as she looks at the Zs in front of them. Heading north was a great idea, and she loves Charlie for coming up with it, but the reality is slightly different. She knows that if they can get ahead of the Zs they'll be in the clear, but with hundreds and hundreds of them covering every inch of pavement for as far as she can see, Stella doesn't know how it will be possible. The dump truck isn't designed for the impacts it's taking.

Explosions erupt ahead as the Humvees push through and each take a side next to the dump truck, PCs on top firing off grenades from their launchers. It thins the herd some, but not enough and within a mile, the dump truck is smoking from under the hood.

"Buzz," Stella whispers.

"I see it," Buzz says, "but ain't a thing we can do 'cept keep going."

"What if it breaks down?" she asks.

"Then we fight our way to safety somehow," Buzz says.

They both know the likelihood of that working with the numbers they still see before them. All the way to the next rise is nothing but wall to wall Zs. Stella does some quick math and realizes that they won't make it another mile before the truck gives out. Apparently, Brenda stole the truck, but never took the time really to get it into shape. Once again, the bitch's short sightedness means the possible deaths of innocents.

"Fucking twat," Stella mutters.

"I was thinking the same thing," Buzz smiles. It's a weak smile and a pained smile.

There's a crunch of metal and Stella looks into the side mirror and sees one of the Humvees veering off the road and into a ditch. Men scramble from the vehicle, their rifles firing, firing, firing, until they are overrun by Zs. Stella is about to look away when the Humvee explodes in a massive fireball, obliterating dozens and dozens of Zs around it.

Which clears some from behind the dump truck, but does nothing for the ones in front. The truck starts to chug along, lurching more than driving, until a massive black cloud of smoke billows out from under the hood.

"Sorry," Charlie says, "I killed us all."

"No, you didn't," Stella snaps, "you gave us a chance."

"I wasn't going to just die in that Reynolds shithole," Greta says, taking Charlie's hand and giving it a squeeze. "Blaze of glory, right? Just like Dad always said."

"Blaze of glory," Charlie smiles at her.

"Wait…what blaze of glory?" Stella asks, shocked. "When the hell did your father say that?"

"He always says that," Charlie smirks, "it's our little joke. Easier to know you're going to die when it's in a blaze of glory."

"I am so going to kick his ass when I see him next," Stella says.

No one corrects her "when" with an "if."

The dump truck slugs along for a few more yards, but then quits and dies. A hunk of dead metal amidst a herd of dead flesh.

Buzz pulls his rifle from the floor of the truck and looks over at Stella. "Ready?"

Gunfire has already erupted from the truck bed and Stella nods, picking up her own rifle. Greta pulls back the slide on a .45 while Charlie smiles as he does the same to his Desert Eagle.

"Where'd you get that?" Stella asks.

Charlie shrugs. "It was in the glove box. Your fault for not looking." A huge grin spreads across his face. "This is going to be awesome. Call of Duty fuck the what."

Stella and Buzz are about to open the doors and jump from the truck when a chime fills the cab.

"Uh…what's that?" Buzz asks.

They all look at each other as another chime sounds then a buzzing and a trilling.

"That's our phones," Charlie says and digs into his pocket.

"Where y'all at?" the text reads on all of their phones.

"Holy shit," Charlie smiles. "It's Critter."

"The Wi-Fi is back up," Greta says then looks at her mother, a wide grin on her face. "Dad."

"That man," Buzz says, shaking his head.

"I love my dad and all," Charlie says. "But is someone going to answer Critter?"

"Almost two miles north of Reynolds Mountain on Merrimon," Stella texts back. "We tried to use the dump truck to get away, but it broke down."

"Don't worry," Critter texts back, "we're on our way in my truck."

"Too thick," Stella responds, "you won't get through."

There's no answer.

The Zs push in at the dump truck, shaking it from side to side. Slowly the gunfire from the bed stops as everyone runs out of ammunition.

"Critter?" Stella texts. "Where are you?"

"Do you feel that?" Charlie asks.

"It's the Zs," Buzz says sadly, as some start to climb up over the smoking hood.

"This is what dad felt like," Greta frowns as she looks into the grey eyes of a Z. "When Elsbeth found him. But we don't have an Elsbeth today."

"No, shhhh!" Charlie snaps. "I *hear* it now too."

"Sweetie, it's the Zs," Stella says, putting her hand on his shoulder.

He shakes it off and glares at her. "No, it's not! Fucking listen!"

Before Stella can reply, a rumbling sound fills the air. They all know it's not a figment of their desperate imaginations because the Zs begin to react and start to turn north towards the sound.

"What the hell...?" Buzz mutters.

The view in front of them is suddenly filled with the sight of a two story, yellow machine. The Zs stumble at it, but the huge wedge welded onto the front just shoves them aside like they are made of snow.

"Dad wondered where that thing went," Charlie says. "He told me about it one night when we were hanging out with some of the laborers."

"That thing is huge," Greta says. "What is it?"

"Yes, Mr. Stanford, where else did you think I was calling from?" she laughs. "I am glad to talk voice to voice. It's something that I have meant to do since you killed our associate, Mr. Vance."

"Oh, right," I say. "Yeah, he kinda brought it on himself."

"That he did, that he did," Camille agrees. "But it still put a wrench in our plans. So did the assassination of President Mondello, although that turned out to be a blessing in a way that I can't quite get into at this very moment."

Elsbeth, Cassie, and the rest of the sisters hurry from the stairwell and shove the door closed. The sounds of wet, undead hands slapping against the door echo across the roof.

"We don't have much time," Cassie says. "Find something to brace this!" No one moves. "What is going on? Did you find the jammer? Why are you all just standing there staring at Long Pork?"

"He's on the phone," John says.

"Talking to Elsbeth's mama," Melissa adds.

The shock of that statement lasts for exactly two seconds then Cassie frowns. "We still need to bar the door!"

"Right," Stuart says, launching into action as he starts kicking free the poles the satellite dishes are on.

Everyone not holding the door closed begins to help, while I keep talking to Elsbeth's mother.

Elsbeth. A very angry woman that is stalking right up to me.

"Give me that," she snarls, her hand out.

"Uh, just a sec," I say, holding up a finger.

"Is she there now?" Camille asks.

"Yep," I reply, "want to talk to her?"

"In a moment," she says. "First I need to tell you why you will convince my daughter and the other girls to get onto the helicopter."

As she speaks, I can hear the sound of rotor blades in the distance. Elsbeth frowns and begins searching the sky.

"Master Sergeant Platt and his Team took something from us," Camille states, "which is unfortunate for you and them."

"Who is us?" I ask.

"You know who we are, Mr. Stanford," she sighs, "The Consortium. Stop wasting time with stupid questions."

When she says the word "stupid", I know for a fact that I'm talking to Elsbeth's mom. The similarity is uncanny.

"What is that, Long Pork?" Elsbeth asks, pointing at the incoming helicopter.

"That's your ride," I say. Her eyes go huge and she shakes her head. "Uh, I'm not sure how keen El is to take a helicopter ride."

"Which is why I need you to convince her, too," Camille says, "or the package Platt took will detonate. Is he there, perhaps?"

"Nope," I say, "he has a booboo and had to stay home from school."

"Ah, the legendary sarcasm," Camille sighs. "It must be exhausting being around you all day."

"That's what I've been told."

"Is anyone from Platt's Team there?" she asks.

"Yep," I say.

"Then ask them what package I mean," she says, "I'll wait."

"I don't need to ask what's in the package," I say, "they already told me. It's a dirty bomb."

All eyes turn to me.

"Exactly," Camille says. I can hear the smile in her voice. "And when it goes off it'll render Asheville uninhabitable."

"Yeah, that's what I hear," I say. "But you don't have it, Platt does. So I'm not getting what you're selling."

"Did you think we'd ever let something that powerful out of our hands, Mr. Stanford? We didn't secure Atlanta by being stupid and careless."

"No, I guess you didn't," I say. "So you're saying you let them steal it?"

"Ah, fuck," John says, "Platt was so right."

"I am saying that, Mr. Stanford," she replies. "And I have the detonator right here in my hand. Since you took down the jamming array, I now have a clear signal to the package. I press this button and Asheville will be a radioactive wasteland. It'll take a couple weeks, depending on weather, but soon your entire area of the Blue Ridge Mountains will be completely unlivable. Unless you like vomiting blood and dying of quick spreading cancers that haven't even been discovered yet."

"I don't like that at all," I say.

the top of his lungs. The three PCs in back are swinging and stabbing with batons and machetes.

The furthest back PC cries out as he's grabbed and chomped on by two Zs at once, each taking an opposite side of his neck. Blood sprays everywhere and the herd goes mad. He goes down screaming for help before his throat is completely apart. None of the PCs even glance his way, they just keep fighting.

Babs gets to the haul truck first and tosses her shotgun aside as an M-4 is dropped down to her. She spins, side-running, and lets loose, the rifle on full auto, as Shots and the other two PCs hurry past her and begin to climb up the ladders onto the platform.

"Come on!" Shots screams.

Babs slams the butt of the rifle into one, two, three Zs, drops it and runs all out, elbowing her way through the sea of undead. She lunges for the ladder, which is just out of reach as the haul truck continues down the street, and she comes up short.

There are gasps and cries from those watching as she is lost under the massive front tire. Many cover their ears, blocking out the sound of her body bursting and bones crunching under hard, vulcanized rubber.

"Jesus," Lourdes says as she looks down on the red smear that is quickly covered in Zs, all fighting for a taste.

"Tough break," Critter says. Lourdes whirls on him, but he holds his hands up. "I say that with all due respect, ma'am."

"Uh, Critter?" Red calls. "Any thoughts on which way to go?"

"Well, Mr. PhD, how about straight?" Critter replies.

"That's going to be a problem," Red says while he drives the haul truck through the herd of Zs, and abandoned cars, shoving, crushing, pulverizing them as he steers the truck down Merrimon Ave to where it becomes Broadway. The distinction line being the overpass of I-240, which still has hundreds of Zs tumbling off the side and down to Merrimon below. "We aren't going to clear that overpass. The truck's too tall."

"Guess we'll need to go around," Critter says.

"Which way?" Red asks.

"Turn at the old Staples," Critter says.

"Nope," Red says, "there's still an overpass that way."

Critter scratches his chin. "Then get up on the highway."

"Come again?" Red asks, looking over at Critter. "You want me to drive into the thick of them?"

"That off ramp is wide enough," Critter says as he points. "Use that, then off road it across. We'll turn on Woodfin and get back to Merrimon that way. BB&T's only two blocks up from there."

"Jesus, Critter," Red says, "this isn't the best idea."

"Didn't say it was," Critter smiles, slapping the man on the back. "But it's an idea."

Red makes the hard left turn, crunching up over an abandoned Prius, and pushes the haul truck right into the heart of the Z herd. Critter nods then leaves the cab, walking over to a ladder that takes him up to the top of the truck so he can look down into the bed.

"Hang on, folks!" he shouts down at everyone. "This could get a might tricky!"

He has to grab onto a rail as the truck bumps and lurches its way through the Zs, then slams into the concrete divider that separates the eastbound and westbound lanes. People in the truck bed cry out in fear, but Critter just smiles, his eyes turned towards downtown. That smile leaves his face in a hurry.

"Well, that ain't good," he mutters as he sees the Blackhawk helicopters heading straight for the BB&T. "Guess we's got ourselves a wrinkle."

"Shit," Lourdes says at his side, "we're close to being out of ammo."

"Get everyone up here that can shoot," Critter says. "Time to lock, load, and pray."

**

"So third floor, east side towards Pack Square," Melissa says. "That's where they'll be." Her phone chimes. "And we best hurry before those helicopters get to us. We'll be sitting ducks in that open bed."

"I took out one," Elsbeth says. "I can take out two more."

"But not before they launch rockets," John says. "One of those and it's all over."

and me and my other arm is just trying to hang onto the rail so I don't fall and get covered by Zs.

Oh, wait, my hand.

I let go and the weight of the Zs takes me down to the concrete landing. I watch as Elsbeth decapitates one, coating me in Z blood, and then kills the other, yet again coating me in more Z blood. Joy.

"Get up," she says and grabs me by my bad shoulder as I try to pull myself up buy the railing.

"AAAAAA! FUCK!" I scream as she wrenches my shoulder.

"Are you hurt, Jace?" Melissa asks, helping me to my feet. "Did one of those Zs bite you?"

"No," I say. Which is the truth. One of *those* Zs didn't. But...

I can see the suspicion in their eyes and neither of them tries to hide the look they give each other.

"I swear on my family's souls that neither of those Zs bit me," I say, "cross my heart and hope to die."

"That's not something to hope for," Elsbeth says, getting right in my face. "So don't say that."

"Aye aye, captain," I say. "Can we go now?"

"Come on," Melissa says and led us down the stairs.

The rest of the group is about three floors ahead of us and we have to jump and hop over Z corpses every step of the way. It's a bit of the apocalypse two-step because not all of the Zs are stilled. Some of them have had their legs and arms chopped off, making them immobile, but still dangerous with the chompers.

I kick in a couple Z faces, careful not to lose my footing in the gunk slick stairs, and stay close to Elsbeth and Melissa. They are busy themselves finishing off the Zs that have taken a licking, but keep on ticking. We're almost one floor above the rest of the team when another scream fills the air.

Then the rage yells hit and the entire stairwell is filled with the sounds of women shouting and bones crunching. I can hear Stuart yelling for them to get control of themselves, but as I look over the railing, all I see are women going all Viking berserk on some Zs.

We race to the next landing and stand there stunned; well, Melissa and I are stunned, but Elsbeth is grinning from ear to ear. So, being Elsbeth, she jumps in. Can't blame her since it looks like so much fun...if you are a rage monster from hell.

A Z arm is ripped right out of the shoulder by Steph a
slams it into the thing's head, again and again. That's a fa
move of mine; beating a Z to death with its own arm. Priceless!

Cassie has a Z by the throat and I can see its skin sloughing c
around her hand, but she doesn't care. She also doesn't care abou
the snapping jaws as she brings the fucker's face right up against
hers so they are almost touching, nose to nose. Then SNAP and the
thing's neck cracks in half. The weight of its body pulls the neck
flesh apart and all Cassie has left in her hand is part of a spine and
the head. Which is still snapping at her. She blows it a kiss then
throws the head against the wall. It explodes like a ripe melon.

Next to her, pretty much shoulder to shoulder, is Brittany. And
that woman is crazy! She grabs a Z by the head then jumps up
against the wall, almost walking across it, coming down hard on
the other side. The Z's head is twisted completely around and then
all I see is her fist come exploding out of the thing's belly with part
of its spine! She yanks back and the Z folds in on itself, but before
it can fully fall, she grabs the head and rips it off then crushes it
against the wall. Holy fuck!

Audrey is right behind and she actually tackles a Z around the
waist, but instead of falling all the way down she uses her
momentum to flip herself over it, landing on her feet with the Z
wrapped in her arms upside down. The thing is thrashing against
her, its jaws trying to bite her calves, but she could give a shit as
she drops onto her ass. Fucking piledriver! The Z turns into a
crumpled mess of bone and blech.

Elsbeth is in on the action, but she's more a blades girl. She
spins and takes off the head of a Z with one blade then splits it in
half with the other. Then she does it again. And again. Slice, pop,
split. Slice, pop, split. Like flicking the heads off dandelions. But
with more gore. A lot more gore.

Down below us is Dehlia, screaming at the top of her lungs
and killing and crushing every Z in sight. She could give a shit
about the Zs that get through and snatch a nibble here and there.
She knows she's done and is all about making a sacrifice count.

I need to pay attention to that.

Stuart, John and Reaper come up behind the women and act as
clean up, while Melissa keeps me back, her eyes searching mine

ntly, waiting for me to crack and spill the truth. That's one
, about surviving a zombie apocalypse, you sniff out bullshit
.. It's what keeps you alive in the first crucial months. You can't
t suckered in by lies or you end up robbed, raped, murdered, and,
well, eaten. So Melissa keeps watching me, hoping the attention
will make me crack.

What she doesn't know is all I'm doing is focusing on the pain.
I'm using it as fuel to drive me to my end goal of seeing my family
one last time. It finally hits me that my true worth is as a sacrifice. I
can't stay with them all, not for long, it's too dangerous and I could
turn at anytime and get all snacky on my friends. Or, God forbid,
my wife and kids. So all I want to do is see them and know they are
going to be safe. Then I'll use my last moments on this planet as
best I can: end this nightmare right.

I don't know *how* I'll end it, but now, finally, I know I *have* to
end it.

Knowing is half the battle, right?

Then the screams below us turn to sheer pain and I glance over
the railing to see Dehlia get wedged into a corner. A Z is at her
throat, and she's able to keep it away, but it's the one chomping at
her belly that's the problem. Her t-shirt is torn and bloody as the
Z's mouth goes to work. For a second she looks up at us, fear on
her face, then it's nothing but determination.

She shoves away from the corner, her knee ramming the Z at
her belly, and she wraps her arms around one then two Zs, as she
rushes towards the railing. A third and fourth Z are caught up in her
embrace and then she's gone, over the railing, falling, falling,
falling, thud.

The cries from the sisters are almost ear splitting and I have to
turn my head away at the anguished violence that erupts. I know
the things are monsters, but I've never seen more anger and hatred
directed at anything in my life. The stairwell is filled with rotten
flesh confetti as hands tear, feet crush, blades slice, and everything
that isn't breathing is ripped apart.

It's all the rest of us can do to keep our footing; there isn't a
single stable place to step. Everything, and I include the walls,
ceiling, and railings, is coated in Z gore. It drips from light fixtures,

188

from doorknobs, from old, useless video cameras- everything. It's like this the rest of the way down.

Then we're there, at the third floor landing.

The sisters are panting, close to exhaustion as the adrenaline that has been fueling them threatens to slip away. A couple of them slap each other in the face to keep fired up, to stay focused, but I can see others start to slack a little. Not Elsbeth, though. No, she takes the lead from Cassie and opens the door, her blade sliding right through the skull of a Z as if she knew it was there.

Another gets the Elsbeth treatment then another. The women crowd in close behind her then fan out as they get into the hallway beyond. Wide windows at the end of the hall illuminate them and all I can see past Stuart and the rest are silhouettes of death and the shadows of blood and gore splattering against the walls. In a different time, it would be considered grotesque, but for me, right now, it's true beauty.

Don't tell Stella.

"East windows!" Melissa yells. "Turn left!"

The women get to the end of the hall and turn left, having dispatched the rest of the Zs that blocked our way. But that's the last we see of them. The entire wall of windows ahead of us explodes inward, showering us with fire and glass.

***

"Well, shit my britches and call me Mary," Critter snarls. "Them's sons of bitches. Move yer ass, Red, we gots some whirlybirds to take down!"

The haul truck passes Walnut St and pushes forward towards the BB&T building. But high above is a Blackhawk, hovering just where Critter needs the truck to stop. Its guns go hot and a thousand rounds a second pour into the third, fourth and fifth floors. The windows are vaporized and sparks and fire flash as the bullets hit the metal frames of the windows and the building itself.

Critter sights then fires his rifle. But misses completely. He sights again just as the Blackhawk's guns whir to a stop. Once more, he fires, but it ricochets off one of the skids. Yet the shot wasn't completely in vain; it did alert the helicopter to their presence.

The Blackhawk starts to turn, the guns whirling back to life.

"Well, shit," Critter mumbles then turns to everyone. "Free rations and drink for a year to anyone that can bring that piece of crap down!"

"Fire!" Lourdes shouts.

It's hard to tell what is louder: the helicopter or the sound of dozens of rifle bolts being pulled back. The Blackhawk's guns start to fire, but it takes it a second to dial in on its target. That's one second too long.

The windshield of the helicopter shatters as round after round is fired into it. The Blackhawk starts to fly back and forth and then its main rotors cut into the BB&T building, sending the helicopter spinning to the ground. It explodes on impact. As do the rockets attached to its skids.

The heat buffets the haul truck and Red shouts from the cab as the glass in front of him splinters into his face. Despite the "safety" element of the glass, it's still deadly to exposed eyeballs.

"Fuck!" Red screams and the truck veers off to the right, slamming into what had been a vibrant café, but is now a graveyard of Zs still wearing pretentious vests and fedoras.

Red is screaming and clawing at the glass chunks embedded in his eyes, when Charlie bursts into the cab.

"I got ya, I got ya," Charlie says and pulls Red from the seat.

"Give him to me," Dr. McCormick says, following Charlie, and lays Red out on the platform next to the cab.

She starts to order Charlie to fetch her kit from the truck bed, but the teenager has turned back around and is jumping into the driver's seat. He doesn't bother to wipe away the glass, and gets some shards in his ass for his haste, but he doesn't care as he stares at the instruments before him.

"How hard can it be?" he asks, then depresses the clutch, pushes the truck into gear, and hits the gas.

The monster vehicle lurches and stutters forward as Charlie gets the hang of the clutch to gas ratio then it starts speeding up. Charlie shifts and gives it more gas. They are only feet from the

BB&T building when the second Blackhawk comes from around the other side. Charlie sees it and narrows his eyes.

"Fuck you," he snarls.

***

My one arm covers my head as I bury my face into the nasty carpet. My ears are ringing and I can barely make out someone shouting at me. I have to say that the zombie apocalypse is hell on the hearing. If I'm lucky, I'll die before I go deaf. Oh, wait, I forgot...

"Holy shit," Melissa says. She's probably shouting, but it sounds like a whisper to me.

As I get to my feet all I see is empty space. Where there once were walls there's just shredded drywall and scorched metal studs. Everything has been obliterated by the helicopter. You see belt guns in the movies and laugh as they tear up cars and other shit, but it's no laughing matter when you're staring the aftermath in the face. It's all fucking gone.

"Straight ahead," Melissa says. "Go! The truck is outside those windows!"

We stumble-run our way through the debris, headed straight for the windows. We can see another Blackhawk, but it's not facing us. Which means it's facing the truck. A truck with my family in it.

"No!" I shout and run forward, grabbing a pistol off Stuart's belt. "NO!"

I start firing, but the magazine is empty, of course. So what do I do? I toss the fucking pistol at the helicopter!

It bounces right off.

So I pick up a hunk of metal.

***

Charlie sees the pistol bounce ineffectively off the side of the helicopter and he frowns.

"Are you kidding me?" he says, then sees his dad standing at the edge of the third floor as he chucks a hunk of metal right into the chopper's windshield.

All three walk to the windows, Platt helped between the two women, and see a row of bulldozers making their way through the herd of staked Zs. Behind them are dozens of men with rifles.

"The basement?" Platt asks. "Help me then you run and don't look back."

"You're my patient," Antoinette starts, but Platt cuts her off.

"And you aren't a doctor," Platt says, "but I am a soldier. The pack. It's downstairs in the sitting room?"

"Yes," Stacy nods.

"Bring it," Platt says, wincing with each step. "You get me into the pool and then go."

"The pool?" Antoinette asks. "I don't understand why you need to go down there."

"I used to come here on my days off every so often," Platt says. "Just sit and study the house. It was an antidote to the depressing image of the row after row of pre-fab military housing on base."

"What does that have to do with the pool?" Antoinette asks.

Platt smiles. "First, it's built deep into the ground. And second, little known fact, is that it's lined with lead."

CHAPTER NINE

"Charlie!" Stella screams. "Charlie!"

"Hold this," Reaper says to Dr. McCormick. "When I pull it free we're going in."

"Can we get to the Biltmore?" Dr. McCormick asks. "Melissa says they have a surgery there."

"It's under attack," John says, holding up his phone. "Platt just let me know. I think the elder Ms. Thornberg is covering her bases in case Platt figures out how to diffuse the bomb."

"We're going to the Bywater," I mutter, my eyes on the body of my unconscious, bloody son.

"Not really the time for a drink, Long Pork," Critter yells from inside the cab, having taken over driving duties. "We're getting the hell out of here and back to my holler."

"What medical supplies do you have?" Reaper asks.

"All of them, of course," Critter grins. "You think the boy'll make it there?"

"If we don't stop," Reaper says, looking at me.

"But the sisters," I say, "we'll leave them stranded at the Bywater."

"They'll be fine," Cassie says from the ladder at the edge of the platform. "They're kayaking down river and will hike into Critter's Holler." She holds up her phone. "Just got done texting them."

"Ha!" Critter laughs. "Like to see them try!"

"I need you to take Greta back to the bed," Stella says. There's a tone in her voice I know well.

"Mom, I'm not leaving…" Greta starts.

"YOU WILL DO AS YOU'RE TOLD!" Stella roars. "ELSBETH GET HER BACK THERE!"

"Yes, ma'am," Elsbeth says. Without another word, she grabs up Greta and leads her to the ladder. The two climb up quickly.

More shots and I see a spark a foot above my head.

"Thoughts on those things?" I ask.

"I'd try to outrun them," Critter says, looking at the dashboard. "Which I could do. This thing is faster than a bulldozer any day."

"Then what's the problem?" I ask.

"Fuel," John replies.

Critter nods. "We have enough to get us to where I park this baby and not a drop more. I take a detour and we'll run out well before then."

I can see the bulldozers getting closer, and the armed men riding on top, as they shove Zs by the dozens out of the way. It was the plan all along- flood the area with Zs, overrun the survivors, then bring in the slow rolling cavalry.

So why bother with the dirty bomb?

"We'll take out the drivers," John says as he grabs the ladder and climbs up. "I'll bet there's more than one good shot back there."

"There's plenty," Melissa says and follows.

"Get up there, Stuart," Stella says. "Get safe."

"No way," Stuart says and takes a knee next to us, his rifle at his shoulder. "My place is right here."

He looks over at me and I nod. He nods back. Nuff said.

**

Men poor into the front door of the Biltmore House, their rifles out and ready. But the first few don't get a chance to use them. Stacy squeezes the trigger of her AR-15 again and again. Her breath is relaxed and controlled as she sights down the barrel, putting a bullet into the forehead of every man that is foolish enough to come at her.

The rifle clicks empty and she has the magazine ejected and a new one in without skipping a beat. More men get cut down quickly. One of the men hits the ground and his hand opens up. A small pear shape falls from between his fingers and Stacy rolls backwards, ducking into the stairwell to the basement.

The world erupts around her and she slams her hands over her ears, losing her grip on her rifle. Helpless she watches it clatter down the steps and bounce around the landing, lost from sight. Her options are to go after it, and lead the men into the basement towards Platt and Antoinette, or get her ass up and fight them off.

Stacy steps from the stairwell, a pistol in one hand and a collapsible baton in the other. She flicks open the baton and starts to run towards the front door. The first few men see this battle crazed woman covered in dust and soot and hesitate.

Not the best reaction if one wants to stay alive.

***

Above me, I hear gunfire ring out, matching what is coming from below. Blood poofs out of the chests and heads of the bulldozer drivers, but their bodies are just shoved out into the throngs of Zs and someone else takes their place, keeping the machines rolling towards us.

Critter grunts and I look over at him.

"Just a nick," he says. I narrow my eyes and he tilts his head to show me the scratch on his neck. "Got lucky."

Bullets bounce around us and I realize the men on the bulldozers aren't trying to shoot us, but are trying to shoot out the engine of the truck: their fire is concentrated on the front grill.

"How much can this thing take?" I ask.

"A lot," Critter says. "The engine is reinforced. So don't worry. This thing is built to take a beating and not stop. Otherwise it'd be useless down in them quarries and shit."

"True," I smile then duck as a bullet flies past my head. "Fuck."

I look down at the road and realize we're going full on Footloose with the bulldozers.

"I'm holding out for a hero," I sing. "I'm holding out for a..."

Antoinette nods, turns, turns back, nods again, then runs out of the pool room. Platt watches her go then pushes the pack along with his foot, too exhausted to bend down and pick it up.

***

The first bullet enters Stacy right above the right breast. Her body twists, but she keeps her feet and lashes out with her baton, crushing the man's skull that holds the smoking pistol. The second bullet hits her left thigh and that takes her down. Her knee slams into the concrete of the Biltmore House's main entrance and she grunts, but doesn't cry out. She won't give them the satisfaction.

The third bullet hits her in the throat just as Antoinette makes it upstairs and gets to the massive doorway. Stacy is hit again in the chest, dead center, and her body spins about. Her eyes meet Antoinette's and then glaze over as her heart beats one last time. She falls forward and collapses onto the floor, another body added to the dozens that she already killed.

Antoinette screams, but doesn't slow down. She grabs up a rifle and sprints past the entrance, pulling the trigger and emptying the gun into the men rushing at the house. They dance and shake as they are hit, but she doesn't see them as she tosses the empty rifle to the ground and runs as fast as she can to the billiards room.

Dashing into the room, she leaps and slides across the antique snooker table, and hits the ground running. Her hand reaches out and she slaps the wall, triggering yet another hidden door. In she goes and takes the small set of steps that leads down to the servant's quarters.

She's down the steps and still moving, hurrying past educational displays of what life was like for the people that used to work the estate during its glory days. She doesn't stop to look at the plastic fruit or empty milk cans; she doesn't give two shits about history right now. Her future is all she cares about

She finds the back doors where suppliers used to make deliveries and lowers her shoulder, slamming into the old wood and snapping the chain that secures the doors. The clean air of summer hits her face as she runs from the house out towards the fields beyond.

She hears shouts and gunfire and knows she's being pursued, so instead of running down towards the river, she turns and heads for the front of the estate.

And the field of undead still standing.

***

"You stupid fuck!" Stuart yells as he drags me to my feet. "You were *trying* to die, weren't you?"

"Maybe," I say as he pulls me along.

The sisters have cleared us a path and are busy keeping it clear as Stuart yanks me along, his fist lashing out at the random Z that get's past the women.

"You selfish son of a bitch!" he shouts.

We reach the truck and Critter is hollering for us to get on since we're wasting gas. Stuart shoves me into the ladder and I cry out, but I climb up, not wanting to take anymore shit from him. I get to the top and Stella is glaring.

"I got it moved," I say. "For Charlie."

"It was a suicide mission," Stuart snarls from behind me. "He was bitten and has been hiding it."

"What?" Reaper asks. "Jace? What happened? What haven't you told us?"

"It was back at the Biltmore," I say, tears filling my eyes. "A Z bit me."

"God," Reaper says. "What symptoms do you have?"

"My shoulder is black and fucked up," I say. "There's pus and shit. I can barely move it."

"I knew something was wrong, but thought it was just the stress," Reaper says. "What else?"

"What do you mean?" I say. "I was bitten, man!"

Reaper's eyes narrow. "Let me see."

"COME ON!" Critter yells from the cab.

"Go," Elsbeth says, "they're on the ladder."

Critter puts the truck into drive and gets us moving. I grab onto the rail as the machine lurches and give everyone an apologetic smile.

"Sorry," I say.

leave? I'm blowing this pack no matter what, so I'll give you five minutes."

"That's all I'm asking too," Logan says, walking down the platform to the pool ladder. "Five minutes. I'll send my guys away and set a timer. If after five minutes you aren't convinced then I'll stand right here as you blow us all to Hell."

"Weapons down," Platt says.

"I'm unarmed," Logan replies, lifting his shirt and turning about. He then lifts both legs of his jeans to show no backup pistol. "Let me bring you the phone and we go from there. That cool?"

Platt thinks it over and then nods. Logan looks at his men and motions for them to leave; they do so in a hurry, none wanting to be radioactive dust. Logan carefully makes his way down the pool towards the deep end, but Platt turns his pistol on him.

"That's close enough," Platt says. "Slide the phone to me."

Logan smiles and bends over, sending the phone sliding across the tile to Platt. Platt picks it up and looks at it for a second before putting it to his ear. He turns the pistol back to the pack, his eyes locked on Logan's.

"Hello?"

"Mr. Platt, sir," Camille's voice coos. "It's nice to speak with you since I've only seen you at a distance on security footage."

"It's Master Sergeant Platt," Platt says.

"Right, yes, my misunderstanding," she apologizes. "You know Mr. Logan there was in the Army. He was a captain pre-Z. I think you two would get along and find you have a lot in common."

"I'm not an officer, I work for a living, so I highly doubt we'd have anything in common," Platt snaps. "Get to the fucking point, lady. I'm not up for chit chat."

"Fine," Camille says, her voice ice and gravel. "I have no intention of detonating that bomb anytime soon, Sergeant. I simply need it to be in Asheville. You let Logan take it and put it where I want and you can go free."

"I doubt that," Platt laughs.

"You shouldn't," Camille replies. "I'll let you go free and join your friends, wherever they may be. I lost contact with them after speaking to my daughter. And after they killed several of my people. Unfortunate, but emotions run high in the heat of battle.

Being a long time soldier, I'm sure you know that. How long have you been in the Army, Sergeant?"

"Twenty-five years," Platt replies, "I'm retiring today."

"I should hope not, Sergeant," Camille responds. "I believe you have a lot to still offer this world. Your skills will be invaluable during the coming months and years."

"You have two minutes, lady," Platt says. "And so far you haven't said anything to make me give a shit about you."

"That bomb is a deterrent, Platt," Camille says, all pleasantries gone from her voice. "There is a war coming and it's about to run right over Asheville. That bomb needs to be there as a buffer."

"A deterrent?" Platt laughs. "I don't know if anyone has told you, but the apocalypse has already happened. There's nothing to deter!"

"You don't know how wrong you are," Camille says. "I plan on fighting for what is left. I plan on fighting for my daughter, whether she wants me to or not. I plan on fighting for those other young women, some of whom still have very influential families...*living families*... that would pay anything to know where they are. As long as there is leverage, Platt, there is still society. It isn't over yet."

"One minute left," Platt says, "and I don't give a shit. Tell me all you want, but this bomb is going off in about fifty seconds."

"That's unfortunate," Camille says. "May I speak to Logan first, please?"

"Sure," Platt says, "knock yourself out."

Platt tosses the phone towards Logan, but the man ignores it and instead drops and slides down the pool to Platt. Before the Master Sergeant knows it, he has a knife buried to the hilt in his gut.

"You could have gotten out alive," Logan says. "You had a choice."

Blood bubbles from between Platt's lips and he grins.

"You had a choice too," Platt coughs and splutters. "But you chose to bring a knife to a bomb fight."

Platt pulls the trigger and there is nothing but light.

***

The ground shakes hard and Antoinette is thrown off her feet and into the water. She coughs and chokes as she takes a mouthful of the French Broad, but she spits it out, gets her footing and wades quickly to the kayak that is slowly floating away. She climbs in and grabs up the paddle.

Behind her, America's largest home crumbles in on itself. Flames reach high into the air briefly before several tons of old concrete and brick collapse upon the conflagration, leaving nothing but black smoke.

Antoinette paddles as hard and fast as she can, knowing that what is in that smoke may not kill her today, but it will kill her at some point. And that death will be slow and painful. She digs with all her strength and is soon shooting down the river, her eyes watching the riverbanks for gunmen, but all she sees are the dead.

The thousands and thousands of dead.

***

Those in the haul truck don't even notice the tremor from the Biltmore explosion. It's hard to notice anything when crushing cars and trucks while speeding as fast as possible down I-40.

"He's not going to make it," Stella sobs. "Please, Reaper, *Alex*, do something. You are a medic; you've treated wounds like this, right? You've had to deal with people blown apart by IEDs, right? *Right?*"

"He'll make it, Stella," Dr. McCormick says. "He's a strong young man. If he wants to live then he'll live."

Reaper doesn't say anything as he studies Charlie's wound and looks at all options.

"You don't know that!" Stella shouts at the doctor. "You fixed assholes, not bleeding chest wounds!"

"Hey, hey," I say as I hold her tight. "This isn't her fault."

"It's okay, Jace," Dr. McCormick says. "I don't take it personally. I'd do anything to be dealing with colonoscopies these days. Compared to the zombie apocalypse, assholes look pretty good right now."

"I'm sorry," Stella says. "I'm sorry. It's just that he was so brave. He was our hero. He can't die." She looks up at me, her pained filled eyes nearly ripping my heart out of my chest. "You would have been so proud of him, Jace. He took over when Red was hurt and just started driving the truck."

"Who's Red?" I ask. Dr. McCormick gives me a look. "Right. Never mind. Wait, when did Charlie learn how to drive a stick?"

"I don't know," Stella says, "but he was amazing."

"That Patel girl," Critter says from the cab as the truck crushes another stray car, along with a few dozen Zs. But those numbers are dwindling and the ride gets smoother as we get further from Asheville. "They were always tooling around the Farm together in an old semi."

"Never knew that," I say. "So he was the hero of the day?"

"He was!" Stella cries, her voice wavering between a mother's pride and a mother's fear. "Then he did the unthinkable, Jace! He shot down one of those helicopters! Shot it right out of the sky!"

"Damn," I say.

"Got a chest full of metal for his trouble," Critter says. "Ain't fair. Not that I believe in fair, mind ya, but that shouldn't happen to a good kid like your boy."

"Critter?" Reaper says. "How much further? I need you to go as fast as possible."

"I'm doing that," Critter says. "But we don't have enough gas to get us all the way. Don't you worry none, 'cause I have my men coming this way. Gonna meet us at the bottom of the hill."

"What's wrong, Reaper?" Stella asks. "Is it the blood loss? I'll give him my blood." She looks at Dr. McCormick. "You did that before with Jace and Stuart. Hook me up! He can take all of my blood!"

"We don't have the equipment here," Reaper says. "We need to get him into surgery ASAP. That's his only hope."

I look down at the still form of my son, covered in his own blood, his skin pale white. You live in the zombie apocalypse and you brace yourself for all kinds of things, especially the deaths of your loved ones. I've gone over a million scenarios in my head of how my family would die. But not one of those scenarios involved

"I'll miss that man. And I know I ain't the only one. Godspeed, Big Daddy. Time to run the big Farm in the sky. I'm sure they could use yer help."

Critter wipes his eyes again and takes his seat with the rest. Melissa reaches out and grabs his hand, putting it to her lips. He smiles at her and puts an arm around her shoulders. Behind him, his nephews lean forward and each give him a pat. Critter looks back and gives them a nod then scans the large crowd.

"Where's Long Pork and Missus Long Pork at?" Critter asks. "They didn't come?"

"Charlie," Stuart says from the other side of Melissa.

"Oh, right," Critter nods.

Stuart stands up and takes a deep breath and walks to the front of the crowd.

"I guess, being the senior military man here, I get to say some words about Master Sergeant Platt," Stuart begins. "I didn't know him as well as I would have liked, but I did know what a true hero that man was. We've all heard the story from Antoinette about his sacrifice. I promise that sacrifice won't go to waste. Before I go on, I want to remind you of the meeting later tonight. I hope y'all can attend. We don't have a lot of time to work things out so every bit of input is appreciated."

Stuart looks out and sees several nods, but also a lot of scared and skeptical faces.

"So, Master Sergeant Platt. Where do I start? Oh, I know. There was this time, just after Jace blew up Whispering pines..."

***

I settle another blanket across his chest, making sure he stays warm as he just lies there, still as a corpse.

Jesus, what a fucking thing to say. Where the fuck did that come from? If Stella had heard me say that she'd have cut my nuts off right then and made me take it back while knocking wood with said castrated handful.

He's not a corpse; my son lives. Although it has been touch and go.

After Critter's men got him up to the holler, Reaper was able to stabilize him. Between Reaper, Dr. McCormick, and a man that lived in the holler and used to be a veterinarian, they got the metal out of Charlie's chest. It took fifteen hours and nearly drained the whole holler of blood. I'm pretty sure there are still people only half full walking around.

I sit down and settle into the chair, trying to get comfortable. Which isn't easy since Stumpageddon is still wrapped tightly to my body. I have to have the dressings changed once a day so the shoulder can be drained. Bits of fractured bone still squeeze out of the drainage holes. Yeah, it's pretty fucking gross, but I'm alive, so I have that going for me.

Stumpageddon? His fighting days are done. I'm going to have to put Mr. Spikey to rest. Dr. McCormick doubts I'll regain any mobility in my shoulder. In fact, she'd like to take the rest of the arm off. I told her I'd think on it. Why ruin such an enjoyable experience like having pieces of bones squirted from bloody holes? I need to savor those moments just a bit longer.

"He'll wake up," Elsbeth says from behind me, pulling me from my stupid thoughts. She drags a chair over and turns it around, sitting down with her arms folded over the back. "He's tough like his mama."

"Thanks," I say. "No, I mean it. I'd rather he be tough like her than weak like me."

"You ain't weak, Long Pork," Elsbeth says. "Just not so bright sometimes."

"That's what they tell me," I say. "You go to the memorial?"

"For a minute. I didn't stay long," Elsbeth says. "The others did. They'll say goodbye for me."

"You don't want to say a few words about your fallen sisters?"

Elsbeth shrugs. "Don't know what to say. I didn't know them, the ones that died. They weren't there then they were then they weren't."

"And you didn't want to say anything about...Julio?" I ask. "You guys were lovers."

"Same thing," she says and snaps her fingers. "There and gone."

"That's life," I say, looking at my son's peaceful face. "One day there, the next day gone."

"Where's Stella? Greta?" Elsbeth asks, looking around. "They weren't at the funeral, neither."

"Asleep," I reply. "Stella was in here all night again and Greta hasn't been sleeping so well lately."

"She having the scary dreams?" Elsbeth asks.

"Yeah. She wakes up screaming and calling Charlie's name. She says all she sees is a helicopter chasing him then, when it finally reaches him, the rotors chop him all up."

"That is scary," Elsbeth nods. "I have one with a tiger and a chainsaw."

I look at her and raise an eyebrow and she just shrugs. We sit there for a while, watching Charlie's chest slowly rise and fall.

"Listen," I start, "we need to talk about your mother."

"No," she states flatly.

"Yes," I insist. "The planning meeting is tonight and we've already lost ten days. Your mother isn't going to let it all go. She'll come after us."

"She can try," Elsbeth says and shrugs again. "I'll be here."

"She's your mom," I say. "Don't you want to find out why she's in charge of the Consortium? Don't you want answers?"

"I have answers," she says, tapping her temple. "And they're mine."

"No, they aren't," I snap. "This is bigger than you, El! We need to know what you know! I've talked with all of your sisters, or whatever they are, and they've given me as much as they know."

"No, they haven't," she says.

"What do you mean? You think they're holding back information?"

"Yes," Elsbeth says.

"Why? Why would they do that?" I ask.

Elsbeth stands up and starts walking away. "Why? Because that's how we are made."

I grab her wrist and pull her back. "Made? What the hell are you talking about? See! This is the shit you have to spill!"

216

"You don't spill shit," Elsbeth says, looking at my hand, which I remove from her wrist, then looking back at me. "Spilling shit would be a mess."

I watch her for a second then smile. She smiles too.

"El, I love you like family..."

"Because I am family."

"And in a family you have to be honest. You have to *trust*. If family is for nothing else, it's at least for that."

Her face changes a million times, as she fights the emotions waging war inside her. She starts to speak, stops, starts again, stops, takes a deep breath and starts.

"Dad?" a weak voice rasps. "Hey..."

"Charlie?" I ask, turning from Elsbeth, unsure I even heard his voice. I tend to hear a lot of voices in my head these days, so I never quite know.

"Yep," he grins without opening his eyes. Then he frowns. "I don't...feel...so...good."

"I'll get Stella!" Elsbeth says.

"No, get Reaper and Dr. McCormick!" I shout after her as she runs from the room. "Then get Stella!"

"I'm...really...thirsty," Charlie says.

"I don't know if I can give you water," I say. "I'd hate for you to spring a leak, Rambo."

Charlie frowns and his eyes flutter open. He squints against the light and looks over at me. "Rambo? I don't know what that means."

"It means," I say as I grip his hand, "that you're a motherfucking hero, bud. I've heard all about what you did. Everyone has. They were going to put up a statue to you if you croaked."

"They were?" he asks.

"No, not really," I laugh. "Who has time to make a statue?"

He smiles weakly. "You sure I can't have some water? My throat hurts."

"Then stop talking," I say. "Save your voice for your mother."

On cue, Stella rushes into the room and I have to hold her back and keep her from grabbing Charlie up in her arms. She calms down and puts her hand across his forehead.

"Oh, my sweet baby," she says. "My sweet boy."

"Hey, bro," Greta says from the doorway.

"Where's Reaper?" I ask. "Elsbeth was supposed to get him first."

"She told me you said that," Stella says, taking time to give me a death glare. "We'll talk about that later."

"Can't," I say, "got a meeting tonight. Sorry."

"Asshole," she smiles.

"A sexy asshole," I smile back.

"Are you two trying to make him sicker?" Greta asks as she shoves between us and leans down and gives Charlie a kiss on the forehead. "Welcome back."

"How long was I asleep?" Charlie asks.

"Ten days," I say. "Scariest ten days of our lives."

"Scarier than after Z-Day?" he asks.

"Way scarier," Stella says. "So don't ever fight helicopters again, you hear me? Leave that to the professionals."

"There are professional helicopter fighters?" I ask. "How do I get in on the gig?"

"You'd never get hired," Greta says. "You'd be more like a helicopter clown, get it? Like in the rodeo?"

"Yeah, I get it," I frown, "thanks."

"Excuse me," Reaper says, "can I sneak in here?"

We move quickly and let Reaper do an examination of Charlie and his wound. It takes about a billion minutes past forever, but he finally turns to us and gives a smile.

"I was able to inflate his lung, and it sounds like it's holding strong, but he's not out of the woods yet," he says. "We'll see how he does when he's up and about."

"How long will that be?" Stella asks.

"Not sure," Reaper shrugs. "I don't have enough experience to know. Maybe a week or two?"

"We don't have that kind of time," I say quietly.

"Why?" Charlie asks.

"Never you mind," Stella says, "you worry about getting better."

She looks at me and is about to speak when Gunga comes running in.

"Uh, Mr. Stanford?" he says.

"Gunga, call me Jace, please," I reply.

"Sure, fine," he nods. "I think we need you outside. A couple people want to say some words about Brenda Kelly and well, it's getting kinda ugly."

"Jesus," I mutter and follow Gunga outside.

We make our way through trailers and walkways, down stairs and ramps, until we are walking into the open valley below all the dwellings secured to the cliffs. I have to catch my breath and steady myself before marching up to the crowd that is busy yelling and shouting. I see Stuart trying to break it up, but he's overmatched by the majority that are spitting curses back and forth with an almost equally vocal minority. Critter is just standing aside smiling, of course.

"Hey!" I shout. "HEY!"

Heads turn and they see me coming. Everyone slowly stops yelling, but they are far from calmed down. I walk to the makeshift podium and look each of them in the eye. Which takes fucking forever.

"Someone wants to say some words for Brenda Kelly?" I ask.

There are nods and grunts and a few shouts (for and against) and I have to hold my hand up to get it chilled again.

"Fine," I say, "I think all the dead deserve some last words."

Everyone, to the last man and woman, is stunned. Guess they didn't see that coming.

"Brenda Kelly was an intolerable bitch," I start, "but she was also one hell of an administrator. Despite being evil to the bone, she did get us through those first few months back at Whispering Pines. I know many of you only met her after coming here to Asheville with Mondello, but let me tell you she wasn't always a disagreeable troll." I laugh. "Well, yeah, she was. But that's beside the point. What really matters is that, in her own warped way, she cared about Whispering Pines and its residents. She honestly did. She worried about them and she fretted about them and she did everything in her power to make the place as secure as possible. Sure, that power warped her walnut brain, but that's what power does."

There are a few grumbles, but they let me continue.

"Deep down I don't think Brenda liked who she had become, even before Z-Day, and she overcompensated for that. I'm just pop psychologizing here, but I think that's the root of it. She backed herself into a corner, which only got worse post-Z, and she didn't know how to get out. She had a lot of hate and anger and that was her go to when pushed to the limit.

"But in the end she did work her ass off for the people she represented. She gave a crap about her responsibilities and duties. As crazytown as that woman was, you couldn't call her a slacker. She was devoted to making sure some semblance of society survived."

The crowd is silent except for a few coughs and sniffs.

"And that's what it's all about, right?" I ask them. "Making sure some semblance of society survives? It won't ever be the same as pre-Z. That's not possible. But it can be good. Well, as good as we can make it. That's why I need every single one of you to be at the meeting tonight."

There are some groans.

"No, no, I'm serious. Brenda would be at that meeting, you know that. Big Daddy would be at that meeting, you know that too. But this isn't about leaders, this is about lives. *Your* lives. We need your input, we need your thoughts, we need *you*."

I nod and walk away from the podium.

"Be there, please. We don't have much time. We never have."

***

Detonation Day plus eighteen.

"I don't like it," I say, "it leaves us defenseless."

"Thanks," Stuart says as we sit around the tables that have been pushed together for our last meeting before evacuation. "Way to make an old man feel special."

"That's not what I mean and you know it," I reply, leaning back in my chair and looking at the other faces that have joined us in Critter's "saloon" to go over the final plans before we leave in two days. "I just meant that with Cassie and the sisters off on their mission, we'll only have Critter's men, John, Reaper, and Elsbeth to help protect us between here and Kansas City."

"Lourdes and her PCs will meet us along the way," Buzz says. "Soon as they scout ahead. Supposed to wait for us just past Knoxville."

"My guys are ready," Critter adds. "Plus you have my other nephews, not to mention my niece."

"And it's not like everyone else hasn't seen some type of combat," John adds. "Hell, your kids can fight like the best of them."

"Charlie isn't fighting shit," Stella says from my side. "He'll be sitting in a backseat with a book."

"With a rifle across his lap," John says. "The kid can shoot. You don't take down a chopper like he did without natural ability."

"He got lucky," Stella says.

"Then he has that on his side," John says. "Just proves my point."

"I don't think it does," Stella frowns.

"Okay, okay, we're getting *off* point," I say. "What I'm trying to get across is most everyone is shell shocked. I don't know how much fight they have left and we have hundreds of miles to cover through a fucking zombie wasteland. I'd prefer if the sisters stayed with us."

"We need the intel," Stuart says, "and they are the only ones that can get it and survive to get back to us. Plus, we told them that if they don't have any new information in two weeks they're to abandon Atlanta and catch up to us."

"El?" I ask, looking across the table at the silent ex-canny girl. "Thoughts?"

"People will fight," she shrugs, "or they die. Anyone that doesn't fight is stupid and stupid should die."

"Great, thanks," I smile, "that helped a lot."

"Listen, Long Pork," Critter says, "you're spooked because Asheville failed. You're taking it personally and talking out your ego. You gotta let that go."

"That was even less helpful than what Elsbeth said," I snap.

"He's kinda right, Jace," Melissa says. "You can't expect to fix everything. It doesn't matter how many people we have with us.

Because once we get out on that road, you won't be able to think our way out of danger. And that scares the shit out of you."

"Stella?" I ask. "A little backup?"

"The radiation levels have risen in the French Broad," Stella says. "It hasn't drifted here yet, but it will. We can't stay, Jace, and getting pissy won't stop that."

"Getting pissy?" I growl. "What the fuck is this? An intervention?"

"Maybe," Stuart shrugs. "How about you give that brain a rest and stop looking at all the angles?"

"You have got to be…"

"Shut up, Jason," Stuart says quietly.

"What?"

"Just shut up," Stuart says.

He sighs and rubs his face. I can see the strain everything has taken on him; the man looks a thousand years older than he did just last year when we were sitting in Whispering Pines more worried about bums trying to get in than Consortiums or trying to move everyone across country.

"You've been a huge part of this group, Jace," Stuart says. "You came up with ideas that no one else could. You'd have made a great city planner somewhere, but this is a military operation. This is convoy tactics. You need to take a step back and listen to those with the experience. If we try to plan for every single contingency, we'll never leave." He leans forward on the table and makes sure he has my attention, which he does. Fully. "And there will be casualties. It'll be impossible to take a group this size nearly a thousand miles and expect everyone to live. That's just not possible."

Stuart leans back and lets that settle in for a minute. It's more unsettling, actually, but I get what he's saying.

"So damned if we do and damned if we don't, eh?" I say.

"Damned if we don't, for sure," Stuart says. "Damned if we do then? No way to know."

"Fine, fine," I say, "I'll let y'all work out the rest. I've planned as much as I can. The convoy will at least be as efficient as it can be. I have that fucking shit organized."

"Long Pork is good at organizing fucking shit," Elsbeth says.

Everyone tries to hold it in, but they burst out laughing. Elsbeth looks around like she doesn't know what's going on, but I see a smile playing at the corners of her mouth. I think she likes her role in this group.

"Uh, Uncle Critter?" Gunga says from the doorway.

"Saloon is still closed, Gunga," Critter says. "Give us a few more minutes, will ya?"

"Sure, right, but..." He trails off and looks back over his shoulder.

"What's up?" Buzz asks, getting to his feet. "You got me worried, little brother?"

Little brother. Always makes me laugh since Gunga is the size of a tractor trailer.

"There's a man here," Gunga says. "A stranger. Just walked into the holler."

"Walked in?" Critter asks, his face clouding with anger. "Nobody just walks into my holler."

"Well, uh, he did," Gunga says. "Ain't no one seen him 'til he was walking up the middle of the field."

"Someone's getting their ass handed to them," Critter snarls. "Fallin' asleep on the job is what gets ya kicked out of the convoy."

"No need for discipline of that sort," a man says as he looks around Gunga's bulk. "I'm naturally stealthy. Been practicing it since before the dead rose."

The man is in his mid-sixties, short, skinny and has only a few wisps of white hair floating about his bald skull. His skin is weathered, like he's spent the past few years outside, which is very possible. His clothes are patched and worn, but surprisingly clean.

"May I come in, gentlemen and ladies?" he asks, his tone that of a kindly professor. Which immediately puts me on edge. "I believe I can help with your situation."

"Sir, I don't know who the fuck you are, but you..." Critter starts.

"Mr. Fitzpatrick, I can assure you I am an ally here," the man says. "One that will prove quite valuable. You are all leaving for Kansas City in two days, yes?" He waits for a response, but gets none. "Yes, well, no need to confirm. I know I'm correct."

There's a strange growling, low and menacing, from the table and I glance around.

Elsbeth.

"You will be crossing several hundred miles, which will be dangerous in of itself, all without knowing what awaits you," he continues. "You are going to a settlement that you think will take you in. Let me be very frank, my friends, they will not."

"Who the fuck are you?" Stuart asks. "And how the hell do you know what Kansas City will do or not do?"

"First, let me address the latter," the man says. "Kansas City, or the Combine, as it was known, does not exist any longer. It has been wiped out, to use a phrase. All that is left is charred earth and the ghosts of thousands. You'll want to adjust your plans and head for Boulder, Colorado, and the Stronghold."

"How do you know this?" I ask.

"That's of no consequence," the man says, waving me off. "What is of consequence is no matter where you want to go, whether it's the Stronghold, the Temple, the Garden, Circuit City, or anywhere else, you will not be allowed in without an invitation." His smile turns and chills run up and down my spine. "Or without an introduction."

"Let me guess," Critter says, "you can get us an invitation to the Stronghold?"

Elsbeth stands up and before we know it, she has her blades out. I didn't even notice she brought them with her.

"Not him," she snarls.

"Oh, my, Ms. Thornberg, I didn't see you there," the man says, obviously full of shit. "How delightful to be in your presence again. Are your sisters here?"

"El," I say, standing up and putting my hand carefully –*very carefully*- on her shoulder. "What's up? You know this guy?"

"I know him," she says, her eyes turning to mine. "He's the Devil."

"Well, that's a bit of hyperbole, I believe," the man chuckles. "I'm just as human as any of you fine folks, let me assure you of that."

Everyone else gets to their feet, their eyes going from Elsbeth to the short, old man.

"I think you should cut the crap, mister," Stuart says, "and tell us who you are before we let our friend do to you what her body language is telling me is going to be something very nasty and very violent."

"Of course, of course," the man says, taking a small bow. "My name is Kramer." He stands straight and locks eyes with Elsbeth. "Doctor Stanley Martin Kramer. At your service."

Elsbeth leaps at the man and it takes every able-bodied person in the saloon to take her down and keep her from chopping the guy up. It also takes all of them to keep from getting chopped themselves.

Not being of the able-bodied ilk, I walk up to the little man and bend down, getting right in his face.

"Who the fuck are you, man?" I ask.

But he doesn't answer. Instead, he smiles at me and begins to hum some nursery rhyme, which sends Elsbeth into an even bigger frenzy.

I take a step back, seriously creeped out, and listen to his humming. Is that…Wheels On The Bus?

What. The. Fuck?

THE END

Z-Burbia will return later in 2014

Made in the USA
Lexington, KY
24 March 2014